BEVERLY KILLS

SEAN MCDONOUGH

D & T
PUBLISHING

Eight years ago, I dedicated this book to my wife Kristy in thanks for her, "two cents."

You've given me a lot more than two cents over the years, dear, but I'm as grateful now as I was then.

Laura,
watch out
for the blonde!

1

BEVERLY

THE PARTY WAS SICK. Bro parties usually were.

Not that anyone actually calls them "bros" for serious. It's just one of those labels that creeps into your head and stays there.

Bro.

Nerd.

Prep.

Hipster.

Victim.

I guess I'm a "hottie." Actually, "so fucking hot" is what guys usually say, but that's an adjective phrase, not a noun.

Sorry, I swear I wasn't trying to sound like a nerd.

Anyway, a couple of us were playing flip cup. Bros vs. Hotties. Alicia led our team off. She's petite so she can't really drink fast, but she always flips her cup on the first try. She's a perfectionist like that.

Lyndsay went next. She can't really chug and she can't really flip either but none of us care that much. It's just a stupid game.

Besides, none of it matters when I'm the anchor.

The boys reached their last man first. I didn't know his name yet, that part would come later. All I knew then was that he was some blonde with a nice chin and an overactive pituitary gland. He gulped his whole beer down like it was a dixie cup. Too bad for his coordination, it obviously wasn't his first dixie cup of the night. He was so drunk he could barely make himself stand upright, never mind flip his cup over before it was my turn to start drinking.

When the chain reached me, I burned him. I downed my own beer in a single gulp, flipped my cup on the first try with one hand, and flipped him off with the other one. Everyone got a kick out of that. Alicia and Lyndsay cheered and jumped all over me in a big group hug. They were my best friends going all the way back to third grade. At seventeen, that was a lifetime.

The guys took the loss well. Once Lyndsay starts bouncing around in a tank top, the guys usually take just about anything pretty well.

Except for one.

Over Alicia's shoulder, I saw the creep I'd just beat to the finish line. Apparently he was the only one of the boys who thought of party games as something to win and not just an excuse to flirt with girls. He sulked into the crowd, shouldering some girl's cranberry who-gives-a-fuck onto her blouse as he stalked off.

That kind of thing's a real turn-on for me.

"God, what's his problem?" I asked. Because that's the kind of thing girls say when they like someone.

Alicia rolled her eyes. Of course she knew him. Alicia knew everyone. "Fuck him. He's got JCHS."

"What?"

"John Carpenter High Syndrome. A tragic, incurable condition that mysteriously ensures a bigger prick but a smaller dick."

"He goes to John Carpenter?"

"Captain of their football team," she said with distaste. "I don't even know who invited him."

It wasn't that out of line for him to be here. Lots of kids who go to REM (Robert Englund Memorial) have friends at John Carpenter.

They're our "rivals" but nobody takes that too seriously. Nobody except Alicia because how are you supposed to have somebody to crush unless you draw battle lines first?

Personally, I think we're all the same underneath.

2

I FOUND him by the bar. We were at a house party but Beverly Hills is that kind of neighborhood. Lots of houses have full sized bars and none of them have parents who card. My hookup for the night was still scowling, but I was going to fix that soon enough.

He was pouring a double shot of vodka for himself but before he could drink it I sidled up next to him and took it from his hand. I knocked back the shot like it was water. Then I leaned forward just so and flashed him a smile that hopefully put a lost game of flip cup back into perspective.

"Hi," I said. "I'm Beverly."

3

His NAME WAS ROB. He made a lot of noise about "drinking with the enemy," but either my tits had transferred to JCH without telling me or he was willing to give peace a chance. Either way, when I hinted that I needed somebody to walk me home it took him all of five seconds to gallantly offer to be my escort.

I graciously accepted and led him on a winding path through LA after midnight. Not that that means anything too dangerous where we were. Unless you're on the main drag, Beverly Hills is mostly quiet houses and closed stores. That's the part where me and Rob were, all by ourselves with nobody for company except the ghost roar of speeding cars and hints of entitled laughter drifting in from the far corners around us. Rob kept trying to put his arm around me and I kept moving casually out of his reach as if I wasn't doing it on purpose. Of course, the more I moved away from him the harder he tried to reel me in. He was so focused on trying to feel the curve of my hip that he never stopped to think about the fact we'd been walking for twenty minutes without me once mentioning where we were going.

Boys, they're always so busy chasing, they never stop to wonder where they're getting led.

"So, where do you live?" he finally asked me. But that was impatience talking, not intelligence.

I giggled and finally let him get his hand around my waist. "We're not going to my house," I said, brushing a long strand of blonde hair behind my ear.

"We're not?" I'd laughed so obviously he felt like he had to smile but this was clearly too much for his one track mind to process.

"No," I said. I turned his gaze to the Baja Burger Hut we were walking past. On the other side of the tall, iron fence there was an outdoor eating area with a few plastic tables ringed around the "Playplace," two stories of plastic tubing with a slide and a ball pit in the middle.

"We're going in there."

"In there?" he echoed. "I don't know if that's-"

I kissed him. Curled my fingernails into his hair. Pressed my breasts against his chest. Let my tongue slide around his. Pulled away before he could appreciate any of it.

"Catch me if you can," I said. Before he could respond, I leapt up, grabbed the curved top of the fence, and hauled myself over with easy grace. I knew Rob was watching, but I was wearing a skirt. I'm sure my grace was the last thing he was appreciating.

I landed with the same agile ease and sprinted for the entrance to the playplace. I could hear Rob call out behind me. "Hey, wait up!" He was huffing and puffing, struggling over the fence with much less ease than I did. I heard an "ow," probably one of the iron points jabbing him in the thigh.

I didn't stop. I reached the plastic entry tunnel and crawled inside. I was gone from sight in seconds but I wasn't worried about him not being able to follow me.

I left my skirt for him to find on the steps.

I was well into the plastic labyrinth before I heard his breathy, childish "oh fuck," as he found my skirt and grasped the implications of it no longer being on my body. I heard him come clamoring in after me.

"Beverly?!" His drunken bellow echoed through the network of tubes. "You'd better not be waiting for me to count to ten!"

I didn't answer, but I left my tank top down the right hand side of a T-junction so he'd know which way I turned. I could hear him clearly. Hands and knees thundering against the plastic, propelling himself through the plastic channel as fast as the blood was undoubtedly pumping in his hard-on.

I left my lacey, black bra for him next. I could tell when he found it because the beat of his hands and knees against the hollow tube got even faster.

I was waiting for him in the ball pit. It wasn't an easy fit, I've grown since the last time I'd been in one of these, but I managed to submerge myself up to my neck in the plastic sea. When Rob finally entered, drunkenness and overeagerness made him clumsy. He stumbled face first into the pit. I watched him grope for the mesh net wall like a drowning man and slowly haul himself back to his feet.

While he clung to the netting, waiting for his head to stop spinning, I rose up from the ball pit. I stood in the orange glow of the streetlights, more erotic than anything he'd ever seen online after his parents went to bed. I was naked except for a black thong. My nipples were already hard in anticipation of what was coming next.

"Robbbert," I called demurely.

He looked up.

I don't think his head ever stopped spinning.

His mouth worked furiously for a moment, trying to say a thousand things all at once. In the end, "Holy shit," was all he could croak out.

It was all he needed to say.

I smiled. I beckoned him forward with one finger, eager to finally stick it in.

The whole time, I kept the nine-inch slicing knife carefully hidden behind my back.

Rob came towards me, already unbuckling his pants.

My smile widened.

When he was close enough, I buried the knife up to its handle in his stomach.

He gasped once.

I pressed my body tight against his. Someone who didn't know what they were doing, a psychotic or a first-timer, would hold the knife with their thumb up and apply pressure from the wrist. I knew better. I gripped the knife with my thumb underneath the handle, the pinkie side of my fist closest to his stomach, and pushed hard from the elbow. The tough meat of his abdominals parted from hip to hip with ease, the same way really rare, thin cut beef just separates beneath a blade.

"Oh," Rob exhaled as the knife slashed loose from his side. He wobbled once and then collapsed in a bloody pile with his intestines pooling between his knees.

I went down with him. I batted red, blue, yellow, and green plastic balls away from his body so I could get a better view of his dying moments. I straddled him and kept stabbing. I pounded the knife into his chest. I tore at the open wound of his stomach until it stretched like the Grand Canyon. I gouged out his eyes. I pulled and twisted and slashed until there were no more blue, yellow, or green balls lying underneath him.

I could feel his erection while I was on top of him. It was still hard against me even as his blood stopped pumping.

He was probably dead before he could appreciate it.

4

I HAD my first kill before my first kiss.

I was eleven. My parents had taken me to San Clemente for a week. It's too small to be a real tourist town but it's beachside, quiet, and very, very beautiful. In the afternoon I liked to take walks by myself. My parents were still getting used to the idea of me being old enough to do anything unsupervised but I had a cell phone by then and they were comfortable enough to let me wander while they sat by the water and got drunk. Besides, it's not like this was Los Angeles. San Clemente, population 64,000, was supposed to be safe.

On that day that would change everything, I had it in mind to make a fire. I'd taken a book of matches from the restaurant the night before and anyone was allowed to use the fire pits by the beach. I gathered up some drift wood and, between that and the matches, I figured I had everything I needed.

I was wrong. Not that you could blame me. I'd never started a fire before. I'd never even thought about it until it became the only thing I could think about. Ever since what my mother called "my womanhood" had started, I felt like there was always this maddening itch that I couldn't quite scratch. Some days I felt it between my shoulder blades. Other times it felt like a piece of sand wedged in the corner of my eye. Some days it was just a nagging feeling that there was something important I was forgetting to do. Always, it was making me feel crazier and crazier. I couldn't sleep. I wasn't eating. I tried to talk to my mother about it once but the conversation turned into an extremely uncomfortable primer about masturbation and I decided I'd rather work out what was wrong on my own than go through that again.

The closest thing I'd ever known to relief was the night before at the hotel bonfire. I sat between my parents and watched the flames grow as the activities coordinator went around handing out s'mores. He tried to hand me one and when I declined he made a joke about girls watching their figure.

He was wrong, I was eating plenty.

I was eating the fire.

I was riveted by everything about it. The uncontrollable movement of the flames, the way the logs went from sturdy brown to fragile grey as they burned, the baking heat that felt like a surprise peek at a power I never even knew existed.

The flames made me feel better but they made me feel worse at the same time because the more I saw, the more I wanted. I stayed up tossing and turning that whole night, waiting for the next day and waiting for a chance to be alone and feel that soothing burning again.

I wasn't getting far. I held match after match to the tip of the wood spars but each one just guttered out. I was just about to resign myself to burning pieces of paper when-

"You need kindling."

I looked up and saw a boy. He was a local. My age, deeply tanned, and stretched out like a rubber band from the beginnings of puberty. He was also blushing a shade of red deeper than any flame I could've made. I didn't have breasts to slack-jaw him with yet, but I noticed right away that he couldn't stop looking at my long, coltish legs.

"I need *what?*" I asked.

He said his name was Frankie. He lived on the other side of the cliff. He and his friends came down here sometimes after football practice. He was a running back. He was really fast. I needed to start with smaller pieces to get a fire going. He could show me how.

I learned all of this in a thirty second, rapid fire speech. I also learned that his face could get even redder.

Not seeing any reason not to, I made a space for him and he sat down next to me. He flinched every time his elbow brushed mine but he wasn't kidding about knowing what he was doing. He broke up some of the small sticks into even smaller sticks and quickly turned my jumble of wood into a large, roaring fire. As the smoke rose, the conversation between us became easier. Having something to do calmed Frankie down a bit. He started talking slower.

And me? I was drawn out by the fire.

I told him about my life. Softball, horseback riding, a thousand other things that used to be important and lately didn't seem to matter much at all. Frankie listened to all of it. He was funny, sweet, and, I couldn't help but notice, really cute. He had freckles and his hair was long in the way that was just starting to become popular back then. I couldn't say I was more interested in him than I was in the fire but I certainly didn't mind having him there with me either.

Of course, eventually the fire started to burn itself out. With it went Frankie's composure. "So...." Frankie began but couldn't finish. He was blushing again. His jaw was working furiously, warring with the rest of him to get out a sentence. "Do you want to take a walk? Maybe get something to eat?" I don't know what he would have done if I said no. Probably drown himself in the ocean.

But I nodded. The fire was dead. I didn't see why not. I walked back towards town with him by my side.

If Frankie had been even a year older, what happened next might have happened differently.

My whole life might have happened differently.

But, what happened was this: Frankie asked me back to his house. I'm sure the plan was to kiss me or maybe even "make out" but Frankie was nervous, shy, and, above all, eleven. Whatever he may have wanted to do, when the moment came he lost his nerve and suggested we go into his garage instead and play "swords" with a pair of metal bats.

Like I said, even a year older and he would never, *ever* have a pretty blonde girl all to himself and suggest that we "play swords." Jesus Christ, if you were even playing swords with your GUY friends at age twelve, you were either a geek or you didn't "play" with girls at all, if you get my meaning.

But Frankie wasn't twelve. He was eleven, terrified of making a move, desperate for a way to stall, and swords was a game that he knew.

I wasn't twelve either. I was eleven, full of feelings and impulses I didn't quite understand, and suddenly thrust into a world of new etiquettes where I didn't know what was appropriate and what wasn't.

So, we played swords. Frankie and I squared off in his garage, holding our bats in front of us with both hands like medieval knights. We swung and stabbed but, of course, every "attack" just bounced off each other's bat.

And it was fun. I liked the fast-paced nature of the game. I thrilled to the simulated savagery and discovered that the reverberations of clashing metal did more to sooth that annoying itch than even the fire did. I heard something in our laughs and gasps of exertion that I also heard singing in the crackle of the fire. In the fire, that song was just a sample on loop. In our pretend battle, the song went on. It got louder. More intricate. Here, in our thrusts and parries, I was filling up with whatever power the fire had only hinted at.

I started swinging harder and the song grew louder with each strike. It built and built until I took a swing at Frankie's head and didn't even pretend like I was trying to miss. He ducked it, still acting like we were playing, but I saw unease flicker in his eyes. That look made my blood race and my palms sweat. I tightened my grip on the bat, not a toy now but a weapon that I never wanted to leave my hands.

Frankie tried to smile at me. I bared my teeth in response, but it wasn't in a smile. I bent at the knees and cocked the bat back. I circled and watched Frankie's movements, looking for openings. Looking for weaknesses.

"Ok, no more. Let's play something else."

I roared and came after him again as hard as I could.

Frankie batted my swing aside, but he wasn't playing now.

"I'm not kidding, Beverly. Stop."

I didn't say a word. I tried to go low, a shot that would have shattered his knee if he hadn't gotten his own bat down just in time.

"STOP!" he screamed.

But I couldn't.

That was the last thing Frankie said specifically to me. After that, he tried calling for help. He shouted for anybody who could hear him that we were in the garage and please hurry, I was going to kill him. When nobody came, he stopped screaming words and just howled at the top of his lungs.

His screams only made it worse (or maybe better. I still don't know) and, besides the screams, there was still the clang of clashing metal as I stalked him around the garage. It made my heart beat faster.

Louder.

Harder.

I wasn't really thinking about what I was doing anymore. I just knew how good it felt to swing at him. Something was building inside of my chest. Mad pleasure and desire and rightness all coming together in an incoherent rush of joy that left me forgetting my own name.

Eventually, Frankie made a misstep.

It was bound to happen. He'd been wheezing for breath for five minutes and that cute, long hair was a sweat plastered curtain over his eyes. The end came when he was trying to dance away from me and stumbled over a coiled garden hose. He lost his balance, stumbled, and his guard dropped just a few inches.

It was all the opening I needed. I lunged towards him and

brought my bat down on his skull like a falling comet. I struck him square in the forehead and the reverberations ran all the way up my arms and left me tingling to the elbows.

His eyes changed the second I hit him. The sweet, fumbling, kind of dumb boy I'd spent all afternoon with was gone. In his place was something newborn and beautiful, something that existed only because I'd swung my arms and birthed it into reality.

Not-Frankie tottered in the silence that followed. I watched him tumble to the ground, empty of everything he'd been only thirty seconds earlier.

As he fell, I realized I was in love with that blank, empty collapse.

I might have been caught then and there, but I'd unwittingly planned the perfect murder. Nobody knew I'd gone to Frankie's house. Nobody in town even knew who I was. The only thing in the whole house with my fingerprints on it was the baseball bat and I took that with me when we left San Clemente the next day.

That spring, I used it to lead our softball team to the state finals.

5

I DIDN'T KNOW what to do with my hair the next morning. Up. Wavy. Ponytail. Ponytail with a strand hanging loose. Nothing looked quite right. I wondered if it had something to do with the static electricity from the ball pit. I was still frowning at the mirror when I heard the bellow.

"BEVERLY!"

I rolled my eyes. "Coming!" I shouted back at my dad.

His face was buried in his iPad when I came downstairs, reading the news off the tablet as if he hadn't been screaming his head off for me a minute ago. There was Canadian bacon on the kitchen table. It was greasy and it's murder on my complexion, but what can I say? I have a weakness. I grabbed silverware and a plate from the cabinet and helped myself to a few pieces.

"What time did you get in last night?" my dad finally asked.

I shrugged. "One," I said. Innocent as can be. No staying out past curfew or gutting brain-dead jocks for me.

My dad set down the tablet and glared at me. The burst blood vessels in his nose made his blue eyes look even sharper. He's a cop and very proud of his supposedly fool-proof bullshit detector. "Three," I admitted sourly.

He just nodded and went back to his headlines. A moment passed in silence and I thought maybe he was going to let me off the hook.

"No car. Two weeks."

I slammed my hands down on the table. "What!?"

"You know what time your curfew is."

"It was the last night of summer vacation!"

"And today's the first day of school," he said. Perfectly patient. Infuriatingly unflappable.

"It's senior year!"

"Colleges take your first quarter grades into account," he replied. "And even if they didn't, a new year means new subjects. Who knows? You might actually be taking something that you'll want to stay awake for this year."

I picked up my knife and fork. "History says otherwise," I grumbled. I didn't see why he even cared so long as my grades stayed up. (I should mention that Alicia and I both had "A" averages. You could get good grades without being a "nerd," you just didn't raise your hand in class and you didn't talk about how much you had to study outside of school. As for Lyndsay.... well, Lyndsay was a sweetheart.)

"It's not your history I'm thinking about. It's your future," he went on, gruff but sage figure he thought he was. "You're going to be applying to colleges in three months and you don't even know what you want to major in."

I rolled my eyes. Here we go again. The second I turned sixteen my dad had started obsessing about colleges, internships, and, above all, What Was I Going To Do With My Life. All I could do was take cover once again behind the shield of teenage apathy.

"Me and like ten thousand other kids," I muttered. I kept my tone low and dismissive but God it was hard.

"They're not my responsibility," he said. "You are."

"Then what do you want me to do?" I asked sullenly when all I wanted to do was scream the truth at him.

"I want you to not be asking me that," he lectured. "In less than a year that's your question to answer and sometimes it worries me how little you've thought about it. I want something to matter to you, Beverly."

I bit my tongue to keep from telling him the truth: that I'd thought about it so little because I knew exactly what I wanted to do with my life the minute I watched Frankie crumple to the floor with the life absent from his eyes.

I was a killer. I loved doing it and I was good at it. All I wanted was to keep doing it and keep getting better at it.

Of course, I couldn't tell my dad any of that. Most parents are full of shit when they say they'll support their kids no matter what they want to do (youngsters out there, say you want to be a stripper or a ventriloquist and see for yourself what happens), but my parents "not approving" was the least of my worries. If I told my dad or anyone else what calling I was actually listening to, I'd be tried as an adult and spend the rest of my life in a prison cell.

But then I also knew what would happen to me if I just stayed quiet and went along with the life everyone had planned for me. Step one, go to a good college. Step two, get some high-paying job I couldn't care less about. Step three, spend the rest of my life in a prison cell.

Frustration raged inside of me. It came on so suddenly and forcibly that I could barely resist the urge to take the steak knife off the table, flay his arm down to the bone with a single, artful stroke and let What I Wanted To Do With My Life run red across the table cloth.

Instead, I took the knife to the ham, pathetic, bloodless substitute that it was, and cut a slice.

"Maybe, I could be a butcher," I said, more to myself than anyone else.

"What was that?"

"I said how am I even going to get to school if I don't have a car?"

"I'll drive you."

"You will NOT," I said, mortified.

"Relax. I'll drop you off a block from the school. Or do you want to ride in the back of a squad car? Go put on some red, you can tell everyone you're a Blood."

I'm much scarier than some gangbanger, daddy. I'm not some low life that just wants money or drugs. There's no reasoning with me. There's nothing you can give me so nobody gets hurt. All that I want is hurt.

I almost really said it. In that moment, I was so angry (and maybe pms-ing just a little) that I opened my mouth to tell him who his little girl really was. The only reason I didn't was because a slamming drawer interrupted our argument before I could.

It was my mom. I'd been so busy arguing with my dad I hadn't even noticed that she'd come down. It was 7:30. To be honest, I was surprised she wasn't already at the office.

Late start or not, I guessed she had something important going on that day. She'd broken out her most overpriced pants suit along with the jade earrings she'd gotten herself for Christmas. Her briefcase was on the counter, undoubtedly packed with millions of dollars' worth of pharmaceutical research. Still, that didn't keep her from pawing through the junk drawer like the missing key to her entire career was somewhere behind a mismatched three of clubs from a deck of playing cards.

That was my mom, there was no such thing as a measured response to a problem. She just threw herself at it frantically until everything that opposed her was smashed guts under her best set of heels. She had her Masters in Economics from an all-woman's college. I imagined she thought all of her professors were very proud of her.

My dad, hair uncombed, still not even dressed in one of his three suits, sighed and set down the tablet he'd bought with Mom's money for his birthday. "Problem, honey?" He said the word "honey" as if it tasted like vinegar.

"I can't find my good slicing knife." She had a Tupperware and the makings of fruit salad on the counter. "It's that cleaning lady, Jerry. She's stealing from me."

"What would Rosa want with one knife?"

"I don't know, Jerry. But it's not here and I can't think of a single good reason why it shouldn't be."

I tried to make myself as small as possible. The handle of my mother's slicing knife was on the side of the 101 Freeway somewhere in Koreatown.

The blade was stuck in Robert Cumming's torso.

I've used her knives before. Washed them carefully afterwards and put them back without her even knowing, but last night I'd either been drunker than I thought or my "date" had an undiagnosed spinal misalignment. Either way, what should have been a clean thrust through meat instead struck bone and broke the blade off at the handle.

"Maybe you put it in another drawer," my dad suggested.

"I've looked in every drawer twice, Jerry. It's not here. What I should do is call the police." She cast a withering glance at my father. "There obviously aren't any real cops here."

He just rolled his eyes. "Don't do that."

"Don't do what, Jerry?"

"Say my name at the end of every sentence. I know who you're talking to."

"Grow up, Jerry."

His phone rang. He picked it up without so much as an "excuse me," a move we both knew would piss my mom off more than any smart comeback ever could.

"Yes?"

And then his brow flattened. His jaw set. I recognized this as his "I'm working now" face.

"Where?" he asked. He listened for another beat.

"I'll be there in fifteen."

He hung up.

"What's the problem?" My mom asked. "Did somebody's purse dog get stolen?"

My dad ignored her. His eyes were set firmly on me.

"Where were you last night?"

"Katey Heard's dad's house. He lives in Redondo." Which we both knew was what I'd told him last night. He was just testing me.

"You didn't stop anywhere else on your way home?" he asked. "You weren't anywhere near Wilshire boulevard?"

"No," I lied. "Why?"

My dad was looking at me like a cop. He was on high alert, ready to call me on even the slightest falsehood. I struggled to keep my expression innocent and slightly confused.

"Did you know a boy named Robert Cummings?"

No matter what, I absolutely couldn't let myself smile.

"A little," I said. I wasn't even lying. "He goes to John Carpenter but I see him at parties sometimes." Also not a lie. "Why?"

"Because I just got a call that his body was found this morning. Somebody murdered him last night."

"*Here!?* Are they sure it's him?"

Whether or not it was really Rob Cummings meant nothing to my dad. My "surprise" meant, where ever I'd really been, that I was safely removed from the whole mess. That was all he needed.

That was all anyone ever needed. Do you want to know why so many teenagers wear black leather or gang colors even though they still ask their parents for a hundred dollars to go shopping at the Grove? In nature it's called warning coloration. Animals make themselves look dangerous when they're actually defenseless the same way teenage "rebels" break windows and vandalize walls. They're trying to discourage attackers because, underneath those bright warning patterns and Hot Topic t-shirts, they're nothing but helpless prey.

Predators don't do that. Not the polar bear in the snow, not the lioness on the golden savanna.

Not Beverly Kilbourne in Beverly Hills.

"You know, you never EVER accept a ride from someone you don't know," my Dad said. "I don't care what time it is, you call me and I'll come get you."

Now, I let myself smile. "I know, daddy."

The most dangerous creatures don't want to be noticed. They

blend in so you don't even know you need to be afraid until it's too late to do anything but spasm in a pool of your own blood.

I never had to worry about police creeping after me because I took basic precautions and because pretty blonde girls have sex in the first act and beg for mercy before they get decapitated.

They're not supposed to be the one holding the machete.

I WOUND up driving myself to school after all. My dad had to go count knife wounds in Rob Cumming's torso and my mom was late for a meeting. Though, she wasn't so late that she couldn't spare a few minutes to point out to my dad who made more money and, if you thought about it, whose time was really more valuable?

That was my mom: Queen of a Man's World. Joylessly dragging herself from one victory to another just so she could let everyone else know how hard it was. I could never look at her without wondering what it was about being miserable that made her so happy.

Maybe it's because she has no choice, a sly voice insisted, a voice that always seemed to make itself known after my father started talking about majors and career choices. *Maybe she never asked herself what she wanted to do with her life and now she's too far down this path to ever get off it. You're not at that point yet. Every road is still open to you. You oughta think about starting down one before you get carried someplace you don't want to be.*

I knew which road I wanted to take. It was lined with dead, skeletal trees on either side and there was always the sound of something stalking through dead leaves, just out of sight.

It was the path that was also blocked by a towering, barbed wire fence.

So hop over it.

Sure, that was easy enough to say. Easy enough even to do if you wanted your path to be touring America in a van or living in a tiny, overpriced apartment and taking black and white photos for a living. When all you wanted to do was slice throats and put out eyes, people were less understanding.

I could keep doing what I'd been doing, let everyone else see the good student, friend, and daughter, and keep the killer only for myself, but even that wouldn't hold after this year. College meant another layer of the lie. I'd have to pick a major I was expected to pretend to care about. Then, I had to pick a career I had to act like I cared about for the next forty years. Jesus, maybe even a husband I'd have to pretend to love. With every layer of what I was expected to be, I could already feel the parts of myself I cared about getting crushed into a tighter and tighter space.

The picking was the worst part. It was a cruel joke. I felt like I was playing a game of Family Feud where I knew the number one answer and wasn't allowed to say it.

Alright, Ms. Kilbourne. The category is: Things That Will Make Beverly Happy For the Rest of Her Life. You have three guesses, let's put a minute on the clock.

Well, Steve. I know killing is off the table. How about family?

Bzz! Your mother thinks "hug" is a financial acronym and your father's a borderline alcoholic emotional regressive.

Well, cry me a fucking river, Steve. How about my friends?

Ohh, closer. Number three answer. You do like Alicia and Lyndsay but let's be honest, they're no substitute for a hatchet, a homeless junkie, and an empty alleyway, are they?

I'll give you that one, Steve.

Careful with how often you say my name, Bev. You're starting to sound like your mother.

Shit, right you are. Let's get on with the game. Any chance a career might make me happy?

I don't know, Beverly. What would you like to guess? Teacher? Ad Copywriter? Chief Financial-

Jesus, forget I said anything. I'm actually starting to suspect you're running a crooked game here Stee... pal.

Well, it's actually your game, you know. I'm just a voice in your head.

That's comforting.

My point is, this is your show. If you don't like it, you can always change it.

Great idea. Except it's not just my show. Alicia's watching. Lyndsay's watching. My parents are watching. I can't be here and not act like the person they expect to see. I wish it was just my life, but the truth is that it's not.

I turned into the school parking lot and stopped thinking about my dead-end future. Between the oblivious stoners, scurrying freshmen, and spoiled kids who think it's your responsibility to watch where they're going, if you're not very careful you're going to wind up with a new hood ornament.

(Which reminded me that I'd had my license for six months and I still hadn't run anybody over yet. I promised myself I'd do that sooner and not later. Someone small I could hit with something really big. A skinny trophy wife with an Escalade. Or maybe a model with a Range Rover.)

But, even as my conscious mind stayed focused on getting through the parking lot fatality free, the downstairs part of my brain was still thinking about the end of my imaginary conversation. This was the basement. The dimly lit cellar of my mind, filled with things that always smelled like blood and never made a wrong decision. Whatever lived down there in the dark rarely spoke in words but, this morning, they had a question for me:

Who says you have to be here?

It wasn't for certain yet. There were still a lot of details I had to work out. But, by the time I got out of the car, I thought maybe I had an answer for them.

A number one answer.

"HEY, BEVERLY!"

I bit back a sigh, briefly considered pretending I hadn't heard her, but finally dragged a smile onto my face and turned around. I was captain of the cheer squad this year, I might as well start accepting my responsibilities now.

"Hi, Molly," I said. I tried to just keep walking but then she was in front of me. All red hair and big eyes and desperation for acceptance.

She also looks like she put on fifteen pounds. But cheer camp was only two weeks ago. How is that even possible?

"Beverly, look what I can do." Molly bent down and performed the amazing gymnastics feat of touching both palms against the floor.

"That's great, Molly."

"I know! I'm getting so flexible!" she gushed. She leaned in conspiratorially, "Pat's *really* enjoying it."

"Good for you guys," I said. To be fair, the fifteen pounds had gone mostly to her breasts and ass. I don't know how much he cared about the gymnastics, but I'm sure he appreciated the extra padding.

"Yeah. So, listen, about the stunts this year-"

I pretended to get a text. "Let's talk about it at practice. Later, Molly."

I kept walking. I heard her say, "Bye, Beverly!" and just waved without turning around. Somehow, that was the girl who was dating our quarterback. I shook my head. She must have given a blowjob like a riptide.

I finally found Lyndsay and Alicia were waiting for me at the courtyard before first bell. By "waiting for me," I mean Alicia was dictating orders to someone on the phone while Lyndsay was sending a text, probably something dirty, to her boyfriend.

Every other table was full, separated by hotness, taste in music, and the custody battles that always happens after an ugly breakup. The only thing everyone had in common, even the kids that dressed like Macklemore, was a silver spoon up the ass.

The three of us were the only ones at our table; but that didn't mean it wasn't full. Perks of being at the top of the food chain. We weren't part of any larger clique because we didn't have to be. You didn't come to us, we came to you if we felt like it and you were damn grateful if we did.

I liked it that way. If I couldn't really be myself with Alicia and Lyndsay, at least I didn't have to pretend I was a surfer or an electronic dance kid. The only common threads between us were hotness and liking each other. Other than that, we were free to do what we wanted- Alicia and her activities, Lyndsay and her sun worship, me and my massacres.

I sat down. Lyndsay finished her text and turned to me expectantly. Completely in her own world, Alicia went on talking.

"-And Allen's dad said he could get us a Steinbeck for the set so that's... Don't worry about the vote, Kristy. Trust me, we're doing *Lofts.*"

Ah, the play. Before the yearbook, before the prom decorating committee, before all other things, there was always the spring musical.

Eventually, Lyndsay got tired of waiting for Alicia to finish. She elbowed her in the side.

"What do you want?" Alicia asked. She looked up and finally noticed me.

"Igottagobye." She hung up the phone. Now both of them were looking at me like I owed them five hundred dollar Amex gift cards.

"....What?"

Alicia rolled her eyes. "Are you going to tell us about him?"

I laughed, finally realizing what they were talking about. "Oh, God."

"How was he," Alicia persisted.

"I wouldn't know."

Lyndsay's eyes got wide. "You mean..."

I held up one finger and wilted it inwards, making a falling slide-whistle sound as I did and confirming her worst fears. Not that she screamed, but they both got a good laugh at my pretend expense.

"So then I tried to help him with a little...." I slid my hand around an imaginary penis and guided it towards my mouth. "And when that didn't work the asshole started cursing me out. Like if I gave a better blow job he'd be all over me. So I told him to go fuck himself and left. Took me forever to get back to my car."

Alicia was unmoved by my plight. "Serves you right for picking a Carpenter boy."

I rolled my eyes. "Come on."

"He's their football captain! You're our head cheerleader! It's like Eleanor Roosevelt fucking Hitler! And Hitler? Better body than Rob Cummings."

I laughed at that one. Couldn't help it.

"If you wanted to have sex," she went on, "That party was ninety percent homegrown guys. Sam Craven was eye fucking you so hard it was making ME sore."

I looked over my shoulder to where I knew Sam was sitting, he and a half dozen other guys with the same spikey hair and too tight t-shirts. He caught me looking and gave me what he thought was a sexy nod.

I turned my back on him without a second glance. "I'd kill him," I deadpanned.

"I heard he's got stamina," Lyndsay said.

"...Not what I meant."

"So he's an asshole," Alicia persisted. "Nobody says you need to like him for more than twenty minutes."

I bit my tongue. It was like talking to my dad. Different questions, but the same inquisition and the same inability to offer any real answers. I looked at my friends and knew what they were thinking. Blonde, sweet, tan, curvy Lyndsay and slender Alicia with the dazzling eyes, long legs, and razor-edged wit.

And then me, more gorgeous than both of them and the only one who still never had a real, semi-long term boyfriend.

Like with my dad, all I wanted to do was stop pretending and tell them I'd never met a cock I liked as much as a twelve-inch butcher knife.

...Ok, maybe not exactly like with my dad, but it led to the same dead end.

"I don't need to like him for five minutes," I settled on saying. "All I need are guys nobody knows so nobody cares when they disappear." There. Honest enough.

"Jesus," Alicia said. "Are we talking about ducking guys you've fucked or hiding bodies?"

Maybe too honest. I scrambled for gossip.

"I don't know about hiding bodies, but did you hear that Jason Cochrane got pulled over with like half a ziplock bag of blow in his car?" I had no idea if that was true or not, but it did the trick. Lyndsay and Alicia were both shocked and intrigued and my fatality faux pas was forgotten in favor of a lively discussion of just how fucked Jason Cochrane was. I can't say it was an interesting conversation, but at least nobody was looking at me anymore.

8

ANTHONY

I COULDN'T STOP LOOKING at her.

I once read an article about pornography. I don't mean I was looking at porn like a normal kid. I mean I read an article about how pervasive internet porn had become and how it was affecting the sexual development of the first generation to go through puberty with access to it. Essentially, teenagers were having trouble becoming interested in "regular" girls when they had 24/7 access to a stream of perfect breasted blondes who didn't object to having sex with the cable guy on the coffee table.

I could see the point the author was making and when I did a little more research (no, not *that* kind of research), I found another point she'd missed. To be exact, I found a slideshow that did a bunch of side by side comparisons. One side was a porn star in all of her unbelievable, incredible, lure sailors to the rocks hotness.

The other side was a picture of the exact same girls without their makeup on.

The difference was night and day. Without the pink lipstick and sultry, beckoning eyeshadow these women couldn't even compete with themselves.

It made me realize that it wasn't just the easy access to the sex that was messing us young guys up. It was everything. The lighting and camera angles that captured even the most awkward acts from the most attractive angles; the scripts where no one ever embarrassed themselves or didn't get the girl they were going after. It was really the same thing that had been screwing people up since that painting of Venus on the Seashell- the ides of an unattainable fantasy as reality. It doesn't do anyone any favors, but the very unreasonable truth is that women in real life are not as beautiful as the ones that go up on any type of screen.

Somehow, Beverly was more beautiful than any Venus or Vivid girl I'd ever seen. She was like the sun to me. The warmth on my face. The light in my darkness.

And, just like the sun, she resided a million miles away from me and I would never, ever reach her in a thousand lifetimes.

That was fine though. We all had our unattainable fantasies. At least I could close my eyes and bask in the warmth of mine.

And that was when I heard the falsetto sigh from behind me.

"Ohhhh, Anthony. Do you think I could walk with you to Science Olympiad after school?" The voice was a freakish imitation of a woman's. It sounded like a dying Disney animal.

No longer unnoticed, I forced myself to turn away from the sun.

And came face to ugly face with my best friend, Curtis. Actually, "best" is kind of redundant since he's also my only friend. My grandma says we remind her of Laurel and Hardy. I can see why. I'm tall, stringy, and pale like something from a black and white movie. Curtis is short, heavy, and has a inexplicable fondness for bowler hats. I actually wish I'd never googled them because now I can't think of us as anyone else either. I wish I could, I'd much prefer to think of us as Jonah Hill and Michael Cera. At least they got the girls at the end.

While I thought about this, Curtis continued his utterly terrifying impression of Beverly.

"And do you think that maybe, just maybe, I could hold your pasty, underdeveloped boy hand?"

I walked inside towards my locker, hoping that Curtis wouldn't follow and I could bang my head against it in peace.

No such luck.

"You're pathetic," Curtis continued in his slightly lower normal voice. "You know that don't you?"

I didn't answer him because of course I knew I was pathetic. How could I not?

"I mean, I look in the mirror. Well, before it shatters anyway-"

I had to smile. Even if I had a thousand friends, I hope Curtis would still be my best friend. Aside from being fat, he's ugly. I mean, really ugly. His eyes are too small, his nose is too big, and he's got terrible acne. Still, none of it bothers him. He's never had a bad day in his life and when you're around him, it's hard to get down about your own problems.

"-I look at this twisted, wretched body and I think 'Thank God, at least I can walk out the door and not be Anthony fucking Kilmeade."

"You can fit out a door?" I asked. "That low fat mayo must be really working for you."

"A-ha," he deadpanned. "A-ha. A-ha. A-fucking-ha. You're funny. Mark my words, that's what'll make Bev get tired of long-johned jocks. Jokes."

"Like you don't think she's gorgeous."

"That's where you're wrong. I think she's fucking hot. When you think a girl's fucking hot, all you want to do is dangle her upside down from a chandelier by her nipples. When you start throwing around words like gorgeous, that's when you want to whisk her away in your piece of crap El Camino for a lifetime of romance and two point five minutes of odd squelching noises."

I opened my locker. "Don't talk crap about my car. She's a lady."

"If that car's a lady then so is the bride of Frankenstein. They're made from the same amount of decayed spare parts. But, while we're daydreaming, it's too bad you and me aren't the main characters of some quirky ABC family show. If we were, we could put our heads together and, quipping all the while, we'd come up with a clever plan to get Beverly's attention and make her fall madly in love with you... Of course, once we stop daydreaming, you're still a twelve pound chess club co-captain and she's so hot I honestly think she's photoshopped. So, my final recommendation is that you wait until she's wearing a skirt, get out your camera phone, and make a private show that you probably couldn't get on the family channel."

"You're a real gentleman, Curtis," I said without doing him the dignity of actually looking at him. I was digging through my locker for an errant worksheet so I didn't see what he was looking at when he said, "Must be. Since I'm about to graciously excuse myself."

Found it. I lifted my head out. "The only thing you've ever done graciously is excuse yourself after too many nacho fart-"

Beverly was there.

Next to me. RIGHT NEXT TO ME.

Good God, you idiot. Of course she is. She always is. Beverly Kilbourne. Anthony Kilmeade. It's this way every year because "Kilfeade" is not a fucking name.

She smiled at me. "Hi, Anthony."

She asked me my name freshman year. It's one of the things I loved about her. Amber Kurtz had the locker on my other side. She's not as beautiful as Beverly but she's still solidly hot and I could grow a second head and she wouldn't even-

You moron why are you thinking about this!? Talk to her. Say something. Anything! It's the first day of school. You have common ground. It's the one day everyone has common ground. Ask what she did over the summer. Ask what classes she has. Do something instead of-

She had her books. "Bye, Anthony."

She walked off without a single glance back. Why would she?

Curtis reappeared. "Oh yeah. She's yours any day now."

I wasn't listening to him. I was watching the way Beverly's shirt rippled with the movement of her waist. I was looking at the small of her back and thinking with the cool dispassion of basic, indisputable fact that if I could walk from room 107 to room 135 with my hand on that small, inoffensive patch of cloth covered skin, then I could be struck dead at the far end of the hall and die without a single complaint.

9

BEVERLY

WE HAD the good luck to all be in the same first period class.

We had the bad luck to walk into the classroom and see name placards on every desk. Assigned seating. Alicia groaned. "Look where I'm sitting," she said. I followed her gaze to her seat, a corner desk flanked by a "Toshiro," a "Chauncy," and a "Milton."

"This sucks," she said.

Lyndsay rolled her eyes. "Get over it, it's not that bad."

Alicia shot her a sour look. "Can't imagine why you'd say that."

Alicia's voice oozed sarcasm and disapproval but Lyndsay didn't take the bait. "I have no idea what you're talking about," she said with exaggerated dignity. She flipped her hair haughtily, held her chin high and walked to, even I had to notice, the seat right in front of the teacher's desk.

I went to my own chair, behind Lyndsay and to the left. Not that I particularly cared where I sat. What was originally going to be an easy first day had gotten a lot busier because of what I was thinking of for next year. I was more interested in everything I had to get done instead of what seat I wasn't paying attention from.

Lyndsay twisted in her seat. "Does my hair look okay?"

"It's fine," I said. I was trying to remember where the Guidance

Office was. Three years here and I'd never felt so emotionally damaged to need to go there. I thought it might have been near the girl's locker room. At least, that's where it would be if the building planner was any good at his job.

Lyndsay turned back around. "You're sure?"

"YES."

And then her boyfriend walked in. "Good morning class," he said. He went to the front of the room and started writing his name on the blackboard. "My name is Mister.... Hughes."

He's never said it but I'm convinced Mr. Hughes was a model before becoming a teacher. He had all of the requirements, wavy blonde hair, broad shoulders, chiseled good looks, a smile that could power a small country and, the clincher, Lyndsay had been fucking him since the end of last year. I would have said something more explicit earlier but, honestly, I still get creeped out just talking about it. I couldn't look at him without feeling like some sketchball from Chatroulette had stepped out of the computer and into my classroom. I'm not a prude, but I see the way he looks at every new class of incoming freshman and it's the same way I look at drunks scattering from a bar after last call. It's the look of someone who's starving but can't decide what to order because everything looks so good.

"Some of you may have had me for biology last year-" I saw Lyndsay uncross her legs. That was why she'd worn a skirt today and also why Mr. Hughes smile had suddenly gotten wider. He was looking her right in the eyes when he said, "-But, if I can play favorites for a minute, chemistry is my real passion."

Jesus. I looked back to Alicia to see if she was as grossed out as I was, but she wasn't paying attention. Her phone was out under her desk and she was grimly ignoring Chauncy, Toshiro, and Milton who were all clearly aspiring biology majors themselves.

That's why it was so weird when this huge grin all of a sudden spread across her face.

I craned my neck, trying to get a peek at whatever Alicia was looking at that had her smiling like that. It was easy to get Alicia pissed off, but excited? I looked around and didn't see Channing Tatum offering season passes to the Pantages anywhere.

My own phone buzzed. I carefully slipped it out. There was a text from Alicia waiting for me. Lyndsay was grouped in too.

Beverly's house. After school.

THE FOUR OF them were artfully disheveled and deliberately posed on a jungle gym so it didn't look like they were posed. They were underfed, pasty, and squeezed into girl's jeans. Staring into the camera, they sounded off:

"Hi, I'm Brucey."

"I'm Wesley."

"I'm Tobey"

"And I'm Zachary."

Then, all together, "And we're the Kincaids!"

Brucey hopped off the jungle gym. By a certain scale, he was the most handsome and thus the obvious spokesman. He pointed a finger at the camera. "And we want to play at YOUR prom."

The scene switched to a twenty something girl with two toned hair, a pierced lip, and, judging by her energy level, a pretty expensive coke habit.

"You heard it here first," she yelled. "The MVC Music Channel and the Kincaids are teaming up to hold the first annual 'Race to Rock at the Prom.' We'll be awarding points to every school in America based on school plays, sports team success, and everything else you thought went out of style with drive-in movies and your

CHAPTER 10 | 37

parents. So dust off those letter jackets because if you've got the points, next year you'll be the one telling that cute girl in the next dorm room how the Kincaids played LIVE at your prom."

A music cue, a Kincaids single of course, played her out. Alicia and Lyndsay kept their eyes glued to the TV until it switched over to a commercial for acne pads. Alicia sat up on my bed. "We have to win this," she said.

"Totally," Lyndsay agreed.

They waited for me to chime in. When all they heard was the scratching of my pen, Alicia craned her neck back towards my desk.

"....Bev?"

I didn't look up from what I was writing. "I'm already cheerleading. I can probably do some other stuff too if you want."

"Please, don't go to any trouble just for us." Alicia said. "It's only our prom. Who cares if we have the most amazing band in the world playing five feet in front of us or if we just have somebody's loser stepbrother with a laptop and speakers."

I shrugged and kept working. "I'm not a huge Kincaids fan." That was being kind. I actually thought Brucey Kincaid sang like someone was pumping a barbed hook in and out of his asshole. I kept that to myself because I didn't value my opinion nearly enough to want to get into an argument about it.

"But," I went on, "They would be better than Mr. Goldsmith and his turntables. Plus, I know we can't drive anywhere without one of you playing *Harvest Hearts* at least three times. So, whatever. You need me, you got me."

Lyndsay mimed clapping excitedly. Alicia wasn't so easily placated. She was looking at what I was working on. "Who gave you homework the first day?"

"No one. I'm doing a college application."

"Now?"

Early action for Columbia is due next month."

"You want to go to Columbia!?"

That was Lyndsay. Her obvious distress made me look up. I

wondered if it was just her being dramatic and then I saw that Alicia was just as hurt and surprised.

"I thought we were all going to UC Santa Cruz," Lyndsay said. "California Gurrrrls!"

Alicia sat up on my bed. "That last part is all Lyndsay, but I do remember making plans for a triple together."

Actually, Lyndsay and Alicia made the plan, talking about how super great it would be to be best friends and roommates. I had just stayed quiet and nodded along until they changed the subject to whether the basketball team or the football team had better abs.

"I know," I said. I'd actually forgotten about the whole thing but, even if I hadn't, I wouldn't have thought it was an actual plan. I just figured it was something to fill in the gap between gossip and boys. Truthfully, it hadn't even occurred to me that either of them would have cared about me wanting to go to a different school than them.

"I just feel like it would be good for me to go somewhere different for once," I said. "You know, get a clean slate."

Alicia snorted. "Clean slates are for fat kids who get skinny and poor kids whose parents win the lottery. What's so wrong with your life that you could possibly need a clean slate?"

She could obviously smell the bullshit but the bullshit was all I could tell her. "It's not about what I want to get rid of," I said. "It's about wanting to make some more room on the slate." My last name on the application was only a ghost of an imprint in the page. My pen had run out of ink.

"What do you mean? More room for what?" Lyndsay asked.

I opened a drawer. Inside, there were some scattered pens, my fake ID, and a well-used meat hook.

"I don't know.... More things I want to do. That's kind of the point."

I took the pen and kept writing.

"Oh, I'm sorry." I didn't have to look up to know how furious Alicia was. "Are there things we're keeping you from? Please, if being our friend is so fucking time consuming just let me know and we'll go to Lyndsay's house."

"I didn't say that."

"No, you just said that you have better things to do!"

I wanted to just ignore her but I found myself looking up from my essay into her thin, red flushed face. I didn't know what to say. How could I when I didn't know what she was so mad about?

You could say that you do have better things to do.

Fortunately, Lyndsay stepped in. "Let's not talk about it now. We've got a whole year before this even becomes an issue. Besides, early action isn't early decision right?"

"Right," I said, jumping at the life preserver thrown to me even though the only reason I wasn't going early decision was because I was still considering other east coast schools.

Regardless, Alicia took the out. "Fine," she relented. "If you're really going to ditch us, let's at least agree to make this year as crazy as possible. Or is that too much of a distraction for you?"

I smiled as widely as I could, even though it felt like there was something twitching in my stomach. "Did you forget who you're talking to?"

Alicia didn't smile back. "I don't know. Who are you?"

Lyndsay had her phone out. Quickly. "Ashley Fox is having a party tonight," she said before anyone could say anything else.

"Of course she is," I said, graciously swimming back into familiar waters.

"That's a start," Alicia said. She grabbed her purse.

"It's Beverly's turn to D-D," Lyndsay reminded.

"It's a start for us," Alicia amended. "Grab your keys."

"I'll drop you guys off, but I'm not going to stay," I said.

Thunderclouds gathered on Alicia's brow. I held up my hands before they could start throwing lightening bolts. "I got in trouble for staying out past curfew last night. I'm not supposed to go out."

"Come on," Lyndsay said. "You can't get out of that?"

"I could, but then I'll be in even more trouble when I don't come home at all this weekend. Alicia, are we still going to your beach house?"

"Definitely."

I shrugged. "Then I'd rather do that."

"So then let's just hang here tonight. We can order Sushi," Lyndsay said. Which was weird because Lyndsay never passed on a party. Even weirder, Alicia was staying quiet which meant she'd go along too.

"Go," I said. "Tomorrow one of you has to come back with a bad sex story."

Alicia hesitated. I know she could hear Ashley Fox's carousel rack of vodka shots calling out to her. "Are you sure?" she finally asked.

"I'm sure," I said. "Come on, let's grab some empty water bottles out of the recycle bin and get you guys something to drink in the car."

"I already have," Lyndsay said. Of course she did. "But what're you going to do?"

I ran my fingers over the handle of the drawer hiding the meathook. In my mind, it was already in my hand. I was already in some dark corner of the city, wrapped in the silence that always hides desolate places in affluent cities.

"I'll think of something."

11

I FELT BETTER on the way to the party. There was no talk of college dorms or expectations dashed, only who was cheating on who, what was on sale where, and what shows were going to be in L.A. when.

A month into freshman year they would have a new third leg to shop and party with and they would see me as nothing but someone to tag in nostalgic facebook posts.

And me? I would be somewhere on the east coast in a city of millions where I was connected to no one. I could apply to summer internships. My parents wouldn't raise a whisper about me staying there year round. My mom would view the expense as another badge of accomplishment for herself. My dad, proud of the work ethic he instilled in me, would bravely bear the cross of only seeing his daughter for one or two weeks a year.

Two weeks.

At most.

"What's so funny?" Lyndsay asked. I just shook my head and said nothing but I was powerless to get rid of the smile on my face.

If I could make it to next September, I would only need to keep my meat hook hidden in a drawer for two weeks a year.

The rest of the time, the rest of my life, it would just be me. I would not make the same mistakes again. I would not try to blend in by being a social fixture. I wouldn't have friends, even as window dressings. I'd smile and chit-chat only enough to secure my veneer of innocence and then skate through a major and a career that demanded as little of my time as possible.

The rest of my time, I would kill.

No one to ask me where I was.

No one to lie to.

I could finally be who I really was.

INTERLUDE ONE:

OCTOBER

George Roth always carves his Jack O' Lantern on the first day of October.

It's a tradition that dates back to when his twin daughters were three. Now, even with both girls adults and far from home, it's a tradition he keeps alive.

With every step of the pumpkin carving process, George sinks deeper into his memories. He scoops out the pumpkin guts and remembers coaching the girls' CYO soccer team. The scent of autumn grass lingers in his mind, fresh as it ever was in his nose.

He carves out the triangles for the eyes and remembers Julia's first date. Remembers Sara buzzing around her sister, helping with her hair and makeup. The girls should have been identical twins, but there'd been complications with the second twin's birth and Sara had come from the womb permanently disfigured by the doctor's forceps. It might have been hard between them because Julia was so breathtakingly beautiful but Sara, bless her, had never been anything but best friends with her sister.

He lingers on every part of the pumpkin's face, enjoying the work. When he finally gets to the mouth, it's difficult to imagine the pumpkin's grin being any wider than his own.

The girl who lets herself in through the back door is smiling as well. The drive from Beverly Hills to Canyon Country was traffic free and she took the whole trip at an easy seventy with the windows rolled down. This far north, this time of year, it gets cool at night and the desert wind has painted her cheeks a rosy hue. She has a scarf on for a little extra comfort.

She's also wearing gloves, but she doesn't have them on for warmth.

The door she comes through is unlocked. George hasn't forgotten to lock it. It's just that it's only seven thirty and this is a quiet neighborhood. A safe neighborhood.

George is unaware that he's no longer alone. He's lost in his memories and the girl creeping through his kitchen moves with the ghostly stealth of a panther.

She has his axe from the backyard. The one he used to cut the logs for the fire blazing merrily in the living room.

George is thinking over the Jack O'Lantern's smile. He's wondering whether or not to give it a tooth or three.

It's a question he considers for another moment, even after the axe separates his head from his shoulders.

The blade is that sharp. Beverly's aim is that perfect. Her swing is that smooth.

George lives long enough to decide that one tooth would be just the thing before his head tumbles free from the clean wound of his neck. His body crumples soon after it.

Beverly stops to survey her work. She never takes trophies. It's not the kind of thing you want lying around the house in case your police officer father checks under your mattress for pot. Good housekeeping aside, she never felt compelled to keep mementos in the first place. Who they were before she closed the story of their lives means nothing to her. Nevertheless, she remembers every detail of every murder she's ever committed.

At night, she relives them the way any artist might relive a masterful performance.

When she's seen enough, she takes the axe with her.

Except, at the door she stops. She's not ready to leave.

She goes back into the kitchen, stepping over George's corpse, and finishes carving the Jack O'Lantern.

She doesn't see why she should be the only one smiling.

12

My LIFE GOT a lot better after I put in the Columbia application.

Obviously, I was still waiting to hear back from admissions but just making the decision, knowing that I was really and truly going to leave California and all the baggage that came with it, made staying a lot easier.

I don't know if they did it consciously, but I felt a shift in my parents too after I told them I wanted to go to New York. My dad got off my back about curfew and picking a major and my mom... well, my mom sometimes actually texted me back within three hours if I had to ask her something.

I was taking it easier too. I actually laughed a little at parties even when I wasn't trying to lure someone aside to a real party. I stopped wanting to strangle Lyndsay every time she had too much to drink and had to be walked home like an unruly puppy that couldn't stop licking things.

Nothing was really different. I still thought most of the people I hung out with were idiots that would benefit from a knife in the throat, and Lyndsay was still the most incorrigible drunk to babysit, but none of it mattered anymore. I was leaving.

Even Alicia's usual pissiness wasn't getting on my nerves anymore.

Today, the reason Alicia was sitting sullenly through lunch and ignoring every attempt at conversation was, once again, the prom contest. There was a big banner on the wall with the header, "You Win When the School Wins!" Below that, there was a leaderboard of the top five schools. REM was behind JCH with 35 points to their 58. Alicia kept shooting venomous looks at the scoreboard as if she could change it by pure intimidation. Finally, she threw her lettuce wrap down in disgust.

"I don't even feel like eating," she wailed.

She didn't see the look that passed between me and Lyndsay. There it was, finally right in front of our faces.

"It's only October," Lyndsay said. Not as much because she cared about the competition as much as we were both desperate to say something other than what was on both our minds. "We've got plenty of time before prom."

She barely heard us. "The homecoming game," she brooded. John Carpenter High was our usual homecoming opponent. "We'll have to beat them at Homecoming. If we don't even the score then..."

The bell rang. The typical reluctant march to class began. We all got up but Lyndsay and I both hesitated. Finally, I sucked it up and said it.

"Alicia, don't you want to eat a little more?"

She sighed and took a single bite from her wrap.

"There." She dumped her almost completely untouched tray into the garbage. "Happy?"

Lyndsay certainly didn't look like she was but Alicia left before either of us could answer. She moved very fast for someone fifteen pounds underweight whose breath had started to smell faintly like vomit.

13

I DIDN'T SEE Alicia again until the end of the day. I was packing my bag, debating whether or not to bring home my history homework or just do it tomorrow in homeroom, when she appeared by my locker.

"So, it's official," she announced. "We're doing *Lofts.*"

"Great, just like you wanted."

"Mhm," she nodded. "Auditions are next Friday...."

I got what she was driving at. "No."

"Beverly-"

"No."

"But you'd make such a great LeeLee!"

"NO!"

I tried to walk away but she'd actually grabbed my purse while I wasn't looking. Now she held it away from me at arm's length like a hostage. "John Carpenter is doing *Fiddler on the Roof.* Do you want their play to be better than ours?"

"You know I don't."

"That's funny, because another blonde said something to me earlier about doing whatever she could to help us beat them." She stroked her chin in mock thought. "Good voice, awesome body.

Can't remember her name though."

"Well, it wasn't Beverly because I'm not a singer!"

"You're good enough to carry a tune," Alicia reminded me.

Fucking West Hollywood Musical Mondays. I knew I never should have let Alicia drag us to that.

"Besides," Alicia went on. "Whatever you lack in classical training, we can compensate with your other..." her eyes dipped to my cleavage. "Natural gifts."

"But there's acting too," I said. "And I've never acted in my life."

Really? A voice that sounded suspiciously like Steve Harvey's said. *Is that so?*

Shut up, Steve.

But Alicia seemed to be thinking along the same lines. "Beverly, do you remember last year? We went to Crystal Lake for spring break but you got all of our parents to believe we were in Springwood, Ohio supporting the Academic Quiz Bowl team?"

I shook my head. "It's not the same." I also made a mental note to see if there were any schools in the Crystal Lake area. I liked it there. It felt homey.

"Except it is," Alicia said. "Beverly, when you talk people just... believe you. And that's all acting is, getting people to believe a lie."

I could feel my resolve wavering. "Would I have to kiss anyone?"

"Just once. And only for dramatic purposes."

I was still going to say no but Alicia saw it in my expression before it could get out of my mouth.

"Just audition," she pleaded. "If there's somebody better I promise I'll pick her. But I need to have the best LeeLee I can find."

It was her eyes that were winning me over more than what she was saying. Her eyes that said no matter how badly she wanted to throw her panties at Brucey Kincaid, the real reason she came to me was because she wanted the play to be great.

Poor bitch. I already knew she was looking at schools with good economics programs for next year. She'd been raised with too much money and status to be anything but a corporate viper. The rest of her life was going to be fifteen hour work days and maybe the occasional play at the Pantages with clients. Maybe she didn't think about it consciously, but she knew this production of *Lofts* with a bunch of overacting drama queens was as far as she was going to go in the theatre.

But her eyes weren't looking that far into the future. Not the rest of her life, not the prom in June, just the one night in April when she was determined to do something she loved as well as she possibly could.

I've looked into the mirror, fresh blood splattered across my shirt, and seen the same eyes staring back at me.

I sighed. Harder than I really felt like sighing, but I might as well start practicing my acting. "Fine. I'm yours."

She let out a squeal that was almost Lyndsay-esque. "Thank you, thank you, thank you." She pulled me into a hug. "I'll get you the songs and we can watch the movie and I'll get a DVD of a live show and..." She kept going on and on.

Behind her, a locker slammed and I saw a blushing figure, who must have been there for the whole conversation, run down the hall as fast as he could.

I guess Anthony was late for a class or something.

14

ANTHONY

"I ONCE HAD POWER, *I was once the man of every hourrrr,"* At least, that's what the last note was supposed to sound like. I had the lung capacity of someone who... well, of someone who hadn't even played a game of tag since third grade.

I pressed on. *"Now nothing's there and I don't knoww, don't know how to fill the airrrr,"* I looked expectantly to Curtis. He was supposed to be filling in the second half of the duet.

Instead, he was sitting on my beanbag chair with his arms folded over his chest. He reached over to my desk and closed the laptop, cutting off the musical accompaniment to the title song from *Lofts*.

"I'm not doing it," he said.

"Just shut up and help me."

"That's exactly what I'm doing." He got up. "I liked *Twilight* as much as the next guy. Actually, no, I didn't. But that's not the point. The point is, being Beverly's boyfriend onstage will do nothing for your chances of boning her offstage."

"Yeah, maybe not." I tried to sound flippant but I couldn't meet his eyes.

"Maybe nothing," he responded. "Also, I hate to break it to you, buddy, but if you want this part you're going to need to have a lot more going for you than looking malnourished enough to have AIDS."

"Exactly," I said. I tapped the sheet music in front of him. "So, from the top."

I went to open the laptop back up, but Curtis grabbed my wrist before I could. I had no choice but to look him in the face now. He wasn't smiling. He wasn't looking at this with the same bleak humor he saw in everything else. No, he had to pick this moment to be a well-meaning bastard.

"Anthony, do you really think this is going to work?"

I didn't need that. I didn't need a sober voice of reality to remind me of my own obscurity. I wanted to be allowed to try. Was that so awful?

Apparently it was.

"No," I said. It hurt, admitting that I was acting like an idiot, but I was able to look him in the eye while I did it. "But, next year I'm going to college and I'm never going to see her ever again. You get that Curtis? Ever." I threw my hands up. "So, fuck it. I'm taking a shot."

Writing it down, it actually sounds ok. Brave and confident and all of the things your parents try to teach you about seizing the day long after they've forgotten what it was like to be a flounder in the shark infested waters of high school. Spoken out loud, in the home stretch of a four year run of humiliation and dismissal, it sounded delusional.

I was lucky enough to escape the kind of relentless torment that drives kids to kill themselves, but I also shouldn't have had any illusions about being able to break out of the box that had been built around me. I was a fucking loser. Forget four years, that had been my cubby since second grade and by now I ought to know it.

And I did know it. That didn't change the fact that part of me still wanted to get into the ring and take a swing, even if I was destined to take a beating.

It was because I loved her. I loved Beverly Kilbourne without ever having spoken to her for more than two minutes. I didn't have to. You can call it puppy love if you want but I believe that the things that make you whole aren't learned over time. They hit you like a lightning bolt the second you come into contact with them. I knew *Supernatural* was going to be my favorite show as soon as I saw the first commercial for it. I read the back cover of the first *Dark Tower* book and I knew I was going to be hooked until the final page.

First day of freshman year, I walked up to my locker and Beverly was there. She thought my locker was hers and she was trying to open it by mistake. When I corrected her, she smiled, said thanks, and went to her locker without a second word.

I fell in love with her right then and I'd only been falling deeper ever since.

Nothing was going to happen between us. I understood that. This was the real world. Self-confidence in spite of all reasonable evidence doesn't help you realize your dreams, it makes you a laughing stock on a nationally televised talent show.

But I had to believe that not all of the people who crashed and burned on those shows were delusional. I had to believe that at least some of them knew how terrible they were but they also knew that they would never accept that that door was closed to them until they ran into it face first.

That was all I wanted. I wanted to get out there and break my nose against unyielding metal so I'd know once and for all that I could never try again.

Instead, Curtis was about to gently and kindly point out to me that the door was locked and I shouldn't even bother knocking. When he did, my pathetic delusion that I could be the male lead in the play, spend three months as Beverly's love interest, and then somehow use that window to make her realize I should be her love interest after the curtain dropped, would be shattered. Then, I'd put the lyric sheet down, we'd play some *Halo*, and my senior year of high school would progress on the same course it would have before I came up with this ridiculous idea.

I waited for him to speak. Whatever he said, it would be enough to destroy everything.

Curtis didn't say a word. He opened up the laptop, turned the song back on, and strutted like a rockstar into the middle of the room, shaking his arms and rolling his shoulders like he was limbering up for a real show.

"I had my chanceeeee to be a starrrrrr, but I looked outtttt and it was too farrrr"

He was belting the notes out like Freddy Mercury. Not exactly the way it was supposed to be sung.

I thought it sounded perfect.

Then I ducked a thrown issue #24 of *The Ghastly Grinner.*

"You missed your cue, you nitwit! Come on, I'm not the one that's going to be doing this in front of people!"

15

BEVERLY

ALICIA WAS right to pin her hopes on the homecoming game. Stupid name aside, the red and green Robert Englund Macaws were almost always contenders for the state championships and last year's JV squad, this year's varsity team, had regularly smacked the crap out of the JCH King Snakes all season.

This year was shaping up to be more of the same. Three games in and our defense hadn't allowed more than one touchdown per game. Pat Raimi, our quarterback, was winning games effortlessly. I mean that, *effortlessly*. He was jogging off the field after throwing four touchdowns a game and he wouldn't even be sweating as he waved to the dozen college scouts in the first row.

I'm sure the crowd that showed up for homecoming expected no different. The sun was bright and warm. It was the perfect kind of day to throw on your "Property of REM Athletics" T-shirt, pack the stands, drink some sodas (maybe mixed with something stronger) and watch a good old fashioned, all-American, massacre.

And, after almost two quarters of play, a massacre was what they were getting.

They just didn't expect to be the ones getting sliced up.

While we'd spent the off-season talking about how good we

already were, John Carpenter High had been working hard with their new football coach. Then, the season started and the whole division discovered that Coach Meyers had silently reorganized the King Snakes into an unstoppable, emotionless killing machine. I was on the sidelines with the rest of the cheerleaders. Other than the players, we had the best view of this new JCH team and it really did look like someone had set a basket of snakes loose on a bunch of defenseless parrots. I saw bulky linebackers fly through the air like they weighed nothing and surefire passes swatted down on every play.

It wasn't that they were bigger or necessarily even better. They'd been made meaner. Savage.

Bloodthirsty.

With a minute left in the second quarter, we were down 35 to 7 and, as another Robert Englund runner got steam rolled, it didn't look like the momentum was going to swing the other way anytime soon.

While they scraped the running back off the field, I led the cheer squad in another vain attempt to rally the crowd. It was an uphill battle when the players' moans of pain were louder than our chants of support.

We finished a set of back handsprings and then two of the girls bent down and cupped their hands together for a Liberty pose. I stepped onto the makeshift steps and waited for the familiar rushing sensation as they propelled me up.

I signed up for the cheerleading squad because it seemed like the right kind of thing to let people see me doing. I only stuck with it for the stunts.

I learned real quick that the uniforms were stupid. And all of the clapping, cheering, and plastered on smiles made me feel like I was an artfully posed mannequin that was screaming on the inside.

But I didn't feel that way when we started flipping and flying and the blood raced in my veins and a single misstep meant a fractured skull.

The girls acting as my base pistoned me upwards. I stood atop the platform of their hands, balanced on one leg with both arms raised and the field and the stands full of spectators sprawled out in front of me.

I loved being lifted. Those moments where I hung in the air, my body perfectly straight and tense, looking down on a crowd of people the way a hawk hovers over a field of mice, those were the moments where I felt completely at peace.

Right now, in the thirty seconds I was elevated, my eyes took in everything. I could see the John Carpenter players pounding fists and jubilantly butting heads.

I could see Coach Haley calling a timeout and our mud and grass smeared players hobbling into the huddle.

I saw Alicia in the stands. She had her phone out and was typing frantically. She might have been looking at the rest of the team schedule. She might have been seeing what other school events qualified for prom points. She also could have been looking up easy-to-brew poisons to slip into the JCH water cooler. Whatever the specifics, it boiled down to the same thing: If we lost, how could we get ahead in the Prom Competition?

I could also see inside the REM huddle. From my elevated angle, I watched Coach Haley gesture wildly and point at things on the clipboard. He was trying to explain some kind of play, but his players looked too battered and shell-shocked to follow what he was saying. They were doing their best though, trying to follow Xs and Os that probably looked like Ys and Qs.

Except for Pat.

Pat wasn't listening. He was looking into the cheerleading section with eyes that were dazed and dreamy because of something other than a concussion.

I followed his line of sight and it led me to Molly. She was duck facing at him and batting her eyelashes in a way that I found sickening but he apparently found a lot more interesting than what was happening on the field.

Coach Haley slapped the side of his helmet, calling Pat's attention back to the huddle.

But, a few seconds later, he was smiling at Molly again.

He'd been doing that a lot, trading kissy faces with Molly when he was supposed to be focused on the game. Up until now, he was so talented that he could afford to be distracted and still burn three quarters of the league. Obviously, John Carpenter High was not in that seventy-five percent, but it seemed like Pat had his head too far up Molly's skirt to notice.

Pat Raimi. Quarterback. Leader. The one who was supposed to hold his team together when things got rough.

If REM wanted to get back in this game, someone really needed to get his mind off of her and back onto the field.

It's a bad idea.

That's not true.

Ok, it's a great idea. But it's also a risky one. There must be five hundred people here. You're asking for trouble, and for what? A game and a prom you don't even care about?

True, I didn't.

But I had interests of my own that I cared about plenty. And, if pursuing my interests just so happened to help out Alicia and the school? Well, then that was a win all around, wasn't it? Everyone gets what they want, and nobody gets hurt.

That's not exactly true.

Well, I guess there was no arguing with that.

Somebody was definitely going to get hurt.

The cheer routine was done. I braced my body for the drop.

And when I landed, I could almost feel the rodent of an idea thrashing weakly in the talons of my mind.

The game went on. Right before half time, the cheer squad was supposed to do another Liberty lift. The girls lined up around me like we did last time but I took a step back.

"Change of plans," I said. "Molly's going to fly this time."

The other girls hesitated, certain they'd misheard me.

Molly didn't. She pushed herself to the front of the group. "Oh my God," she squealed. "Are you serious!?" She looked like she was ready to fly without help from any of us. Still, no matter how high she was already flying in her imagination, the look that passed between the other girls flew way over her head.

I knew what they all were thinking. Molly was a good twenty pounds heavier than me and she wasn't very well-coordinated either. She'd trained to do all the stunts, just like the rest of us, but the most basic aerials were still way beyond her and I usually relegated her to background clapping duty for anything but the simplest routines. Really, the only reason she was even on the team was that her father was an agent at UTA. A happy daughter meant plenty of generous celebrity guests at every school fundraiser.

It was actually kind of funny. Looking at the other girls I didn't realize there were so many different ways for eyes to say, "Beverly, what the hell are you thinking?"

What I was thinking was that Molly already had the star player's attention. She might as well do something useful with it. But I ignored the other girl's questioning looks and smiling at Molly like I had pom poms made of pixie dust that would magically keep her flying ten feet above the ground. "Mhm." I told her. "Let's take it from the top. Molly, you're going to be the big finale." I grabbed her by the shoulders and maneuvered her into the position for the start of the routine. I wasn't rushing too much, as the hobbling REM offensive line was still limping off the bench. We started our routine as they hobbled into position.

"R! E! M!" Each exclamation point came with a clap. We started in two lines, shaking our red and green and flashing our pearly whites. "CAN! WE LOSE!? IN! YOUR DREAMS!" I smiled and cheered with the rest of them but I was also careful to keep an eye on the field. Pat was crouching down behind his players, getting ready for the snap.

It was time for the big finale. I took my place as Molly's left leg base. The other girls kept their smiles on for the crowd, but up close you could see how anxious they were as they followed my lead.

Molly stepped up into the stirrups of our hands. She almost fell just trying to get into position, but she managed to windmill her arms and keep her balance. The only one who couldn't feel the tension was Molly. She gave us a go-ahead thumbs up. She was ready.

We propelled her up as one. For a shining moment, Molly was queen of all she surveyed. In the crowd, her parents saw her and lost their minds with excitement. Her dad even put down his cellphone.

On the field, rather than calling for the snap, Pat looked up at her. His eyes widened in adoration as Molly raised her fists high over her head, transforming herself into a triumphant, bronze idol.

My grip below her foot wavered.

My palm barely twitched. Any of the other girls could have kept their balance. If it had been me I wouldn't even have noticed the shift in my footing.

Molly could barely stay vertical on a wet floor.

She swung her arms once, fighting to stay upright, and then she fell.

A gasp rippled through the crowd before she even landed, a single massive intake of breath and fright. Pat dove forward as if she could be caught like a dropped pass.

She couldn't. She hit the ground and a fault line made of blood cracked its way along the length of her skull. More blood flowed out, drenching her red hair until it was even redder.

And that's when the screaming began.

16

I WAS HOLDING my breath as the paramedics rushed over to Molly. They shouted for us to stay back but, of course, everyone crowded around her. I wound up next to Brittany Lopez, who was supposed to be Molly's spotter. She kept sobbing and apologizing for what happened. Who she thought she was apologizing to, I have no idea. Molly was just so much twitching, broken toy on the floor. And even if she was conscious, one ear was mashed into the grass and the other was so clogged with blood that she couldn't hear a word.

But, if Brittany was talking to me, I would have told her she should be fucking sorry. No one expected her to defy the laws of gravity, but, Jesus, we went over this incessantly. She should have at least tried to break Molly's fall or cushion her head or do SOME-THING other than just spot the place Molly was going to crash land.

Luckily, even if Molly couldn't fall gracefully she at least had a hard head. Whoever was in the booth was too morbidly focused on the "accident" to stop the clock and the halftime buzzer sounded just as Molly was carted off of the field in critical but stable condition. Once she was gone, hushed chatter rippled through the stands. A few minutes later, Principal Vernon's voice, trembling but trying for strength, echoed over the field. He announced that Ms. Cyrus was injured but she was expected to make a full recovery and, after the half time break, the game would resume on schedule.

I exhaled. *Thank God.* Coach Shipman called us all together for a pep-talk and I disguised my relief that everything had worked out as gratitude that Molly would be ok. I actually hadn't meant for Molly to land headfirst like that. The game could continue if a cheerleader left with a broken leg. A dead girl would have sent us all home.

What mattered was that the game would go on. And, more importantly, it would go on with the quarterback actually paying attention to what was happening on the field.

At least, that was my plan when I sat Molly down on the wall and set her up for a great fall. I figured without Molly's tits waving hello to him from the sidelines, Pat could go back out and play without any distractions.

Instead, with five minutes before the game was set to resume, there was some commotion going on in the huddle of REM players.

I didn't know what had started it, all I knew was that Coach Hayley was squeezing Pat's shoulder supportively and then Pat was unsnapping his helmet and jogging back towards the locker room.

What the hell's wrong with him now?

I jogged after Pat, mindful of the clock steadily ticking towards the start of the third quarter. Pat's backup was only second string quarterback because we didn't have a third string to stick him on. If he was leading the team, they might as well not bother coming out.

I caught up with him in the parking lot. "Pat, where are you going?"

Up close, I could see that he was crying. Tears ran down his cheeks and his normally tan face had turned an ugly yellow color. "After her. Molly. Jesus, I can't just leave her alone! I have to- to-"

Sit in a hospital waiting room for six hours? Even if I wanted to ask, the sobs were too thick in his throat for him to answer. Two minutes to go and I needed to pull him together. I didn't understand this. With Molly out of the way he should have been fine.

But he wasn't fine. His eyes were squinting shut as another truly unattractive sob ripped through him. He pushed past me.

"I have to go. I need to be there when she wakes up."

I grabbed his shoulder.

"Pat."

He stopped. His eyes unscrunched and then cleared. He looked deep into my eyes, and froze in their depths.

Spoken for or otherwise, no man ignored me once I wanted his attention.

"You've got a job to do," I told him. "We need you to win this game. Molly needs you to win this game."

"Molly?" he asked. It was as if for a moment he'd completely forgotten who she was.

"Molly," I repeated. "You're her white knight. Her champion." He remembered now. And he wasn't frozen either. He was burning. Whatever love he felt for Molly was feeding off the fire I was building inside of him.

"If you leave now, that's not how you'll be going to her," I said. "When she wakes up, do you want to be able to put the game ball on her night stand? Or do you want to give her nothing?"

Pat shook his head. "No." His hands knotted into fists. He looked back at the field and I almost saw steam coming from his nose. "Hell no," he said.

"Good." I put his helmet back on. I didn't kiss him but I leaned in close so my lips were just on the other side of the face guard. I let him see a little of who I really was. I let him overload on beauty and hunger and intensity until I could feel the desire raging inside him. Then I aimed it where I wanted.

"Win," I whispered.

Pat ran back to the field. He rejoined Coach Hayley and the team a second before the whistle blew to resume play.

I went back to the cheerleading squad. The girls were shaken, some of them still had spots of Molly's blood on their skirts, but they were starting their routine like they were supposed to.

The King Snakes roared back onto the field. They were the same unstoppable juggernauts they were before the "accident."

The Macaws were the same battered, weary bunch of kids that they were going into half-time.

Pat was not the same.

He wasn't a high school senior walking onto a football field anymore. He was a titan striding out to war.

They lined up. No huddle, no play calling. Pat just wanted the damn ball.

"HIKE," he bellowed.

He got the ball a second before his defenders crumpled. The JCH blitzers swarmed him before he could take a step.

The crowd was already groaning in disappointment before they realized that Patrick Raimi wasn't going down.

He should have been. Tacklers were wrapped around his legs. Others were driving shoulders into his upper body, trying to topple him.

Pat didn't care. He freed one leg. Then the other. Two hundred pound bulls were still throwing themselves at him but Pat batted them aside like nothing.

He started to run. The crowd was going insane, cheering and chanting his name as he juked and zipped around midfield defenders with a speed and grace he hadn't shown all game.

Pat crossed the thirty yard line like a rocket. The twenty. Defenders were still chasing him but nobody was even close.

The only opposition left was the safety waiting at the five yard line. He'd had the time and distance to track Pat's run and plot an intercept course. He was also huge enough for JCH to entrust the entire end zone defense to him alone.

Pat saw him coming and didn't care. The two of them slammed into each other, helmet to helmet, with a resounding "crack" that you could hear clear across the field.

The JCH safety dropped like he'd been stabbed. Pat took the hit without flinching and stomped a cleat print in his chest on the way to the end zone.

Crossing that white line was like the clock striking midnight. The demon who roared across the field disappeared and Pat was just a teenage kid again. He spiked the ball and basked in the adoration of the home crowd. They were screaming and jumping up and down in their seats as if the game had already been won. Which, in effect, it had. Pat was no longer the God of War I'd made him but after the run he'd just made the momentum was firmly on our side. The rest of the Macaws were rushing in to hug Pat. On the other end, the King Snakes were showing something that I hadn't seen in their body language all afternoon.

Doubt.

It set the pace for the rest of the game. John Carpenter High was never quite able to rebuild their juggernaut and Pat would go on to lead Robert Englund Memorial to a victory in the final seconds of the game.

Up until now, I've described the Macaw supporters cheering as if they'd won the game after every achievement. When they actually did win, there was no describing it. Their cheers set off car alarms in the parking lot. They picked Pat up and didn't just carry him off the field, they carried him all the way to the after party.

I watched all of this from the silent alley of the entryway to the locker room. I did not join those howling their victory to the cloudless afternoon sky. I didn't want to.

I wasn't proud of my part in helping the REM Macaws snatch victory out from between the King Snake's fangs.

I was proud of the red spots still staining my white shoes.

INTERLUDE TWO:

NOVEMBER

A month later, she is still thinking about the homecoming game.

She has replayed her conversation with Pat Raimi in her head a dozen times over and it still confuses her. If asked, she would describe it like finishing a book and still not quite understanding the plot.

Pat lived for football. She knew that. He had ambitions of starting for one of the division 1 college teams and then getting pulled early in the NFL draft. He drilled incessantly even after practices were done. He didn't even smoke weed because he didn't want to risk damaging his lung capacity.

So why would he abandon all of that to sit bedside with a girl who wasn't even conscious to blow him?

It confuses her. Beverly understands passion. She understands talent and hard work and dedication to your calling. What she doesn't understand is what could make someone set all of that aside for nothing. They called Pat gifted, but she knows from experience that if you have a gift, there's no setting it aside. If you try to return it or leave it unopened under the bed, then that gift will rip itself free and choke you with ribbon until you acknowledge it.

Could it be love? Not as she always understood it and dismissed it, but the kind of all-consuming love you see in animated movies and teen romances. Beverly always thought all of that Nicholas Sparks bullshit was pathetic, but she wonders now if she was too hasty. She wonders if it's possible to truly love someone so much that you'd trade away everything else that gives you purpose, everything that defines you, just to spend another hour with them.

She thinks of the boy currently writhing underneath her. The two of them are parked on a hill high over Hollywood, passionately trading caresses of hands and tongues. Or, at least enthusiastically trading caresses. The boy she's with cares nothing for her as a person. The only thing he wants is the feel of her body against his.

She imagines that he does want more though. She pretends they're in love. They hold hands at the movies. He's listed with a "<3" next to his name in her phone. Her online profile is a towering monument to "Love You, Baby." She imagines caring about him so much that she would give up anything and everything to be with him.

And then she draws the butcher knife from her purse and stabs him through the mouth with it.

She's fast enough that he can't stop her. Slow enough that he doesn't die instantly. The tip of the knife is small enough to fit cleanly into his mouth but it widens towards the handle. She pushes deeper, puncturing the roof of his mouth. Deeper still, and the widening blade cuts into his gums and lower lip as well. The blood fills his mouth, overflows, and runs down his face.

He is still alive for all of this. He looks up at her with eyes wide with terror, confusion, and agony.

Beverly looks back at him, still imagining that she loves him, and is unimpressed.

Her love did not slow her hand. Did not affect her unerring accuracy nor dim her joy at the hot blood soaking her hand.

She puts all of her muscle behind the knife and the point pierces through his brain pan. The boy's body starts to writhe and buck uncontrollably.

Beverly is still straddling him. His death thrusts are the first pleasure she's taken from his movements all night.

When she gets out of the car, the windows are steamed over from the pants of passion that passed between them. Him for her, her for his death.

She pauses to bend down and inspect her reflection in the side view mirror. Her hair is mildly tousled. She fixes it before throwing her hip into the back bumper of the car. The car is in neutral and the hill is a steep one. Momentum quickly claims it.

Beverly doesn't bother to watch as the vehicle speeds towards the bend in the road. She knows what will happen after the car smashes through the guardrail and into the chasm beyond it, just like she knows no one will be able to pull any trace of her presence from the wreckage.

She is not thinking so much about Pat and Molly anymore either. They've fallen from her mind the way any story will after it's been deconstructed and found lacking.

17

AUDITIONS for the play were in November. I still didn't want to do
it, but I'd been dutifully looking over the musical and I walked into
the auditorium (There was a scoreboard hanging off the balcony
here too. Homecoming had put us ahead of JCH by fifteen points)
with my audition song committed to memory. I hated to admit it,
but I'd caught myself humming it the other night when I was
walking down to the LA river to throw away a meat cleaver. Maybe
it was just brainwashing, but it actually wasn't a bad play.

I still didn't want to be in it though.

I'd at least gotten Alicia to agree to call me up last. I was hoping
that somebody would wow her before I could but, midway through
the auditions, she leaned over to me and said, "You could be an 800
pound mute transvestite and you'd still be my best choice for
LeeLee."

I was still clinging to thin hope but, sitting in the back row with
Lyndsay and Alicia and watching yet another bad Lea Michele
impression, I knew that she was right.

I know what you're thinking, that in Los Angeles there should be
no shortage of decent aspiring stage talent. And you're right, but the
problem is that anyone with even an ounce of talent is either

working full time and getting tutored on-set or, if they have only half an ounce of talent, then they're doing shitty low budget plays in shitty low budget theaters in West Hollywood. Either way, the school play is where you go when no other home will take you in.

This latest singer was so bad that even Lyndsay had to weigh in. "Cast this girl, and whoever wrote this'll be spinning in their grave."

"Tina Thompson," Alicia said automatically. "And she's not dead."

"Don't let her see this if you want her to stay that way," Lyndsay grinned.

Alicia wasn't grinning back. She was biting her tongue. Literally, biting her tongue. I was her secret weapon for a lead but there were still plenty of other roles to fill and precious little talent to fill them. I could see Alicia mentally calculating how much acting spackle she needed to patch her beaten up wall of a play and I could see her coming up short. Lyndsay, cheerfully oblivious, was unaware she was tempting a raging bitch tornado to come down and demolish her trailer park.

Alicia tried to settle down by focusing on her casting notebook but, as it often did, her acid tongue snaked out from between her teeth. "Don't you have to be statutorily raped somewhere?"

"John's coaching football practice until five," Lyndsay said, missing the thinly veiled insult as if it were cloaked in army camouflage.

"You mean, Mr. Hughes?" Alicia asked.

"I only have to call him that when we're in bed."

Alicia shuddered. Lyndsay caught that one on face value. "If he wasn't a teacher, you wouldn't have a problem with it."

"Except he is. And even if he wasn't, I'd wonder what damage he's hiding if he looks like that and he's still fucking girls who can't get their own liquor."

Lyndsay didn't say a word. Her face got hotter but the air around her got colder. She grabbed her bag and stomped out of the auditorium without a look back.

I got up after her. "Lyndsay!"

My only answer was the slamming auditorium door. The singer

onstage gave me a death glare for interrupting her aria but, lucky for her, she found her mark and resumed singing before that look cost her her eyeballs.

When I got back to the seats, Alicia could only shrug. "One of us had to say something eventually."

"You could have used a little more tact."

"If you asked Lyndsay what tact was, she'd tell you it's what you use to put up a poster if you don't have tape."

"She doesn't need to be smart to feel it when someone's trying to hurt her." I'd killed enough idiots to know that.

"If she's our friend and she's not as smart as us, than sometimes we have to think for her," Alicia said. "I don't know why you're bitching at me. I know you think their 'relationship' is creepy too."

"Of course I do. But if it's what makes her happy then it doesn't matter how wrong anybody else thinks it is." I wouldn't realize until much later how defensive I sounded.

Alicia rolled her eyes. "Whatever. She'll forgive me when she needs someone with decent grammar to forge an absent note. Come on, sit. I'm about to audition your last potential love interest." She raised her voice. "Anthony Kilmeade!"

I seriously thought I'd misheard her until Anthony actually walked out on the stage. I mean, to his credit, he'd made a (mostly vain) attempt at looking cool but his composure stopped at his collar and shirt cuffs. His face was bright red and his hands kept fidgeting as he debated where it would be acceptable to leave them. He finally settled on a limp wave. "Uh... hi." His voice was the same quiet murmur I was familiar with. I had no idea how he was going to be able to sing.

Alicia didn't seem too optimistic about him either. She'd opened her phone. "Whenever you're ready, Anthony." She wasn't even looking up.

Anthony jumped when the music started. He stared out into the crowd but his jaw looked wired shut. I expected him to scurry off stage at any second, perhaps muttering an apology too low to be heard. It was bitchy, but I had to smile a little at the thought.

He was taking one step to the side when his deer-in-headlight eyes happened to meet mine. There was a beat when we looked right at each other and he froze in a wide-legged stance that made me smile a little more. Here was the deer waiting to get smashed by a truck.

Then, in a move that turned my smile into an "o" of disbelief, Anthony opened his mouth and stopped that truck right in its tracks.

I rose from nowhere and I started to climb,
No one told me so but I'm saying it's my time
Forget about where I was...

Maybe it was my low expectations, but he actually wasn't half bad. I'd watched the play enough times to know how the song was supposed to sound, and Anthony's pitch went up and down when it was supposed to and his voice actually had a strange, whispery appeal to it.

Alicia wasn't looking at her phone anymore. "What do you think?" she asked.

I shrugged. "You're a better judge than I am, but he doesn't sound terrible."

"Compared to the tone deaf feebs I've been getting all day, he's Phillip fucking Phillips."

"Really? That's who you're going with?"

"I'm being realistic. And he's skinny enough to have AIDS, which is perfect. Think you could stand to be around him for a few months?"

"Yeah, sure. I already know him. His locker's next to mine."

"And you don't have to worry about him hitting on you nonstop, which is another plus."

"What do you mean?"

"Bev, you don't see it? The guy's a nine point five on the 'I Love Dick-ter' scale."

"Anthony!?" He never seemed gay to me. Then again, I could tell you if a person was getting ready to run by the bend of their knee and I could figure how many stabs it would take to bring a man down based on how quickly he could devour a steak; but, for all of my honed hunting instincts, my gaydar was terrible.

I looked at him more closely. Onstage he was gesturing wildly to go along with his singing. None of his sweeping movements really said "Man, I could sure go for some raw steak and tits right about now."

Still, there was something about him that just....

"Really?" I finally said. "You think so?"

"Seriously? If you're going to be this fucking dense you don't get to help me think for Lyndsay anymore."

"I just don't see it!"

"Listen, has he ever hit on you?"

"No."

"Ever 'check his phone' with the camera lens conveniently pointed at you?"

"I've never caught him."

"Then he's gay. What else could it be?"

18

ANTHONY

THE FIRST CHANCE I GOT, I was going to steal one of those posters and frame it on my wall.

There was nothing even remotely romantic about it. Beverly and I weren't even photoshopped into the same sections of the poster. Our heads were the biggest, but we were staring morosely in opposite directions with miniature cutouts of the entire cast sandwiched between us.

I didn't care. Just seeing my name next to hers, again and again on the "Coming Soon" posters plastered all over the school, was enough. I couldn't seem to pull myself away from the sight, even after Curtis appeared behind me and clapped me on the shoulder with his usual over-exuberance.

"Congratulations," he said. "What the fuck do you do now?"

I shook my head, still grinning despite the stinging handprint now branded between my shoulders. "I have absolutely no idea."

"You seem ok with that," he remarked.

I shrugged. "I honestly didn't think I was going to get the part. Anything that happens now is just achievement points."

"I'll tell you, buddy, nobody hated your chances more than me. But now?" He started shaking me like a manic father who'd just seen his kid hit a game-winning homer at a little league game. "I think we need to get some lottery tickets because the universe might just be on your side!"

That was a comforting thought. I wasn't being modest when I told Curtis I wasn't expecting to get any closer to Beverly even if I did get the part. My philosophy now was to just enjoy whatever I got and not complain about what I didn't. Still, I sure as hell wanted the ride to last so, if Curtis was right and the celestial forces of reality wanted to get behind me and push, well, I would take all the help I could get.

Curtis nodded down the hall. "Of course, if you wanted to test that theory, you could go down there and see if Beverly wanted to join you for a celebratory milkshake down at The Hop."

I'd been so focused on poster Beverly that I hadn't even noticed the genuine article at the far end of the hall. Beverly was leaving the building with Alicia and Lyndsay on either side of her. Beverly was trying to talk to both of them but neither one seemed that interested in talking to each other.

Not that it mattered to me. Maybe the universe was stacking the deck in my favor, but that didn't mean I was about to go all in after winning one lucky hand.

"Even if we had somehow been transported back in time to 1953," I said to him, "I'm sure she's got better plans."

19

BEVERLY

WE HAD family dinner that night.

I don't have much of a sense of humor. I don't watch any sitcoms or late-night animation and I make up an excuse not to go when my friends want to see a comedy in theaters. If I'm with a group, I usually just feel out when something's supposed to be a joke and chuckle along when everyone else does.

So it's a little unfair that family dinners are the one thing I find absolutely hilarious and I'm not allowed to laugh. At least, not out loud.

It's always my mom's idea. "Dinner" is usually my mom getting takeout at the office and Dad coming home with a bag of whatever he grabbed on the road. The more pissed he is at my mom, the greasier the bag is. All I have to do is swing down the stairs, grab whatever he picked up for me, endure a brief interrogation about my hopes, dreams, and daily routine, and run back upstairs before Alicia or Lyndsay signs off G-chat. If dad's working a night shift, then I'll take advantage of the lack of supervision and hit Compton with a strip of barbed wire for some soul food and some food for the soul.

But, every now and again my mom will read something about

how degrading it is to assume a career woman can't have time for a family and she'll mandate four or five days of Family Dinner to prove a point. That lasts for about a week and then I'll ask what time I need to be home and mom'll just say, "Big presentation next week, tell your dad to get you something."

Until then, I get the side-splitting hilarity of watching my parents try to carry on a pleasant conversation like they have any feelings for each other than dislike and contempt.

Tonight, there was a new gag. My dad was late. Usually he'll play along until my mom loses interest in the idea, but this time he was a solid half hour late and hadn't answered any of my mom's texts. I didn't know what she was saying, but with each message she punched the screen of her phone just a little harder.

He finally came in. He hung up his coat, entered the dining room, and went straight to the liquor cabinet without a word.

"Sorry I'm late," he said after Mom had stabbed so many daggers into his back that he finally felt one.

"It's alright, Jerry," my mom spat. "It's not like we waited for you or anything."

He held up his drink. "You see this? It means I don't need any whine with my dinner."

He sat down. "How was your day, Beverly?" he asked before my mom could get in a comeback. This was his new go-to tactic. Rather than engaging my mom in a fight like she wanted, he'd taken to smothering her at every turn.

"Alright," I said. "Alicia talked me into taking a role in the school play." I was grinning. I tried to play it off like excitement for the part and not glee at watching them both sharpening their knives.

"Really? That's great. Who're you playing?"

"Leelee." That was Mom. She cut me off before I could answer. "It's one of the leads. If you'd been home on time you would have heard when I asked."

"Oh, so you remembered to ask about her day?" He threw his arms up theatrically. And a little wobbly. I suspected the brandy wasn't his first drink of the evening. "She can answer e-mails, approve magazine ads, AND still find the time to ask her daughter basic questions about her life! Is there anything this woman can't do!?" He ignored the food in front of him in favor of another swig of his drink. He'd poured five fingers and was already down to two.

"Well, Jerry," she said. If the drink wasn't cold enough, I'm sure the way Mom was glaring at him was icy enough to bring it down a few degrees. "I already make most of the money. If you don't think my parenting skills are on par with yours, maybe you should stop playing cops and fucking robbers with your friends and Beverly can just call you 'mom'."

"She might as well. You've already got my balls."

"No, Jerry. That would imply you had balls to take." She threw her fork down, hard enough to take a chip from the corner of a hundred dollar plate, and stormed off without another word.

I was alone with my dad. Show over.

This was new. Had my mom.... quit? In the ten years since their marriage had dissolved into an endurance cruelty contest, I'd never seen my mom once walk away until she'd gotten every ounce of blood from my dad that she could.

As comedy routines go, it wasn't the funniest I'd ever seen. I looked to my dad to see if he was as surprised as I was.

He just took a bite from his plate as if mom had never even been there.

"So, it's almost December. How's senior year going?"

INTERLUDE THREE:

FEBRUARY

Zac Ferrera likes to think of his girlfriend Anna Murphy as a treasure that fell from heaven.

Of course, he's fifteen-years-old and in love for the first time. Expressions that people who've experienced more of the world might think of as naïve (not to mention sickeningly sweet) strike him as completely and unironically accurate. But why shouldn't they? Experience is just a better branded word for pain and Zac has never been hurt. At least, not by Anna. As far as he's concerned, the two of them are in the opening act of the greatest love story that's never been told.

Like all great love stories, theirs is not without its drama. Anna's father is a Vice President of Development at Warner Bros. and her mother runs the Los Angeles office for one of the largest real estate companies in the country.

Zac's mother is the Murphy's housekeeper. She lives in Pico-Union but her employers agreed to let her list their home as her official address so she could get her son into a better school district. Anna's parents don't mind. The boy's quiet, earnest, and it's an easy Social Crusader merit badge to boast about at cocktail parties.

The result of this arrangement is that Zac often goes to Anna's house after school and does his homework in the kitchen while his mother scrubs floors that cost more to install than they pay for rent every month.

The result of Zac coming over to do his homework is that he and Anna fell in love.

Nobody can know. The Murphy's enlightened attitude extends far enough to grant a hardworking, underprivileged, minority student an education but stop well short of letting said student within breathing distance of their daughter. Zac's mother wouldn't care who her son was dating but the Murphy's would fire her for Zac's transgressions and she would very much care if her son was jeopardizing their livelihood for a girl he likely wouldn't even remember in a year.

None of this means anything to Zac and Anna. Zac loves Anna for her intelligence and imagination. Anna loves Zac's kindness and quiet determination. They've sat together beside her pool, legs dangling in the water, and traded stories. Anna's told him about the guilt she still feels for abandoning a true friend for the sake of being popular when she was eleven. Zac's told her about tucking his pajamas into his socks so rats won't crawl up his legs in the middle of the night. He's helped her with her math homework. She's helped him with literature when his still-developing English wasn't up to the task.

Eventually, they shared their first kiss beside that same pool.

That was almost a year ago. Now, Anna's parents will be at some party all night and Zac's creeping into her side yard in the fading light of sunset. He lied to his mother, skipped out on soccer with his friends, took three buses to get to her house, and has never once questioned if it's worth it.

He has flowers and wine with him. Valentine's day is not for another week and a half, but Zac has no way of knowing if they'll be together for the day so he's decided to surprise Anna by making every day they're together Valentine's day until the fourteenth passes. And if they should actually be together on the Valentine's Day? Then he plans to tell her for the first time what they both already know.

He's going to tell her that he loves her.

But right now that thought is as far as it can ever get from his mind. He's not yet old enough to drive, but he understands that a single sloppy step could spell disaster for both of them. So, for the moment, he puts his overwhelming feelings of love aside in the name of survival. As he works his way to the backdoor, Zac's eyes dart in every direction. He's looking around to make sure nobody's there to mistake him for a home invader or, worse, anyone who might recognize him as that nice latino boy Ed and Sara took in.

When he's satisfied nobody's out in their backyards to see him, Zac dashes for the back door. He glances up. Anna's window is open, just like they agreed.

"Anna!" he hisses, trying to be just loud enough for her to hear him, low enough that nobody else does, and wishing once again that he could afford a cellphone. Then, he waits for Anna to toss the backdoor key down towards him.

He doesn't have to wait long for something to come out the window. But, it's not a key dropping down into his waiting hands.

It's Anna.

She crashes down on top of him. Her body hits his as if she were so desperate for his embrace that she threw herself out the window rather than wait for him to climb the stairs. Her chest is ripped open, as if she were inviting him to reach into her ribcage and take the heart that belonged to him since the moment they met.

But, if Zac has any opinions about what this all looks like, he'll never get to share them. He's brain damaged when Anna's skull smashes into his. He's killed when he crumples beneath her weight and his already cracked skull shatters against the stonework and a dozen bone shards riddle his brain.

Beverly looks down at their remains from the third story window with more satisfaction than any Juliet could feel at the sight of her Romeo. It's a shame these people are total strangers to her. If she knew that Zac liked to describe his girlfriend as a blessing that fell from the sky, the irony might have been enough to boost the smirk on her face to a full blown smile.

It's a smile she could have used. Beverly doesn't know it yet, but February is going to be a month of precious little joy.

20

GOING INTO FEBRUARY, we'd manage to increase our lead over John Carpenter High to one hundred points to seventy-six. You'd think that would give Alicia an excuse to relax for one day, but she'd been dictating orders sourly into her phone ever since we sat down. The cafeteria had been decorated with a bunch of hearts for Valentine's Day. I kept checking to see if any of the ones around her head had turned black.

"Don't worry about the money, Vanessa. I'll square it with Mr. Campbell. You just find someone who'll rent us an old Bolex. The fucking thing doesn't even have to work."

While Alicia couldn't stop talking, Lyndsay was just quietly poking at her food and not really talking to me either. I didn't mind the quiet. The memory of the two kids I'd killed the weekend before was fresh in the theatre of my mind and I was happy to rewatch the show. A second victim appearing out of nowhere while one is still warm right in front of you is better than putting in one quarter and getting two gumballs.

"Vanessa. VANESSA. Go to AFI, find some hipster who thinks 'film's just so much more real,' and fuck him for his if you have to.

Just don't bother me with this shit. If you can't do the job I'll find someone who can."

She hung up and dug into her food. Half a burger and a fistful of fries disappeared like a magic trick. Stress eating.

"Problems?"

"Nothing I can't handle."

The rest of her burger disappearing said otherwise. She turned to her fries or, what was left of them, and said, "So, you want to tell us about it?"

Was my smile that obvious? I was about to say, "tell you about what?" before I realized she was looking at Lyndsay and not me. I still almost said, "tell us about what?" before I took a closer look at her myself. Her shirt was on backwards and the tag was poking out from the neckline. God, I thought. Mr. Hughes again. Then I noticed how red her downcast eyes were. She'd been crying and she didn't have the usual broken jaw grin she came back with after a stolen period with him.

Lyndsay just stared into the tabletop as if she hadn't heard her but Alicia wasn't about to let it go. "Lunch is only forty minutes, Lyn," she said impatiently. "You want to spit it out or not?"

'WHY?!" We both jumped. Half of the cafeteria turned around. I didn't know Lyndsay had that kind of volume inside of her.

"Lyndsay-"

"WHY!? JUST SO I CAN HEAR YOU SAY HOW RIGHT YOU WERE?!"

She switched off then. She lumped down in her seat and her head rolled to the side listlessly. With all of the people I've seen die, I'd never seen the life just disappear from anyone the way it ran out of Lyndsay.

Then, she put her head down on the table and started to weep. The bubbly, sweet girl that always clogged our newsfeed with silly memes and clickbaits had become nothing but a mass of knotty, blonde hair trembling under the storm of heartache raging inside it.

When she started crying, Alicia and I were too stunned to do anything. Then, a new expression slowly came over Alicia's face. It wasn't a good one.

She moved beside Lyndsay and started to stroke her hair. "It's ok, honey. It's ok." She was trying to sound soothing. With Lyndsay's head down, maybe she even did. But I could see Alicia's face and the barely disguised vindication there painted her words with an ugly brush.

I was the only one who seemed to notice that the whole cafeteria was looking at Lyndsay and a lunch aid was coming over to see what the problem was. "Come on," I said. "Let's go to the bathroom."

We had to pick her up out of her chair. We almost carried her, still bawling hysterically, out of the cafeteria. As we reached the door, from the corner of my eye I saw another girl get up. Allison Hale. The snooping bitch had waited until she thought we wouldn't notice to start trailing us, undoubtedly beside herself at the thought of all the juicy gossip she could gather.

I waited until Alicia got Lyndsay into the bathroom and then I spun around and caught Allison red-handed as she opened the bath-room door. Her eyes widened in surprise. She really thought I hadn't seen her.

I fixed Allison with a glare that's usually the last one a person ever sees. "Come into this bathroom," I told her, "And I will cut your fucking head off."

She froze in place and turned a shade of cottage cheese white that didn't go with her outfit at all. I slammed the door in her face.

Inside the bathroom, Lyndsay was still sobbing and Alicia was still comforting her-slash-waiting to hear how right she was. "It's alright, Lyndsay. We're here. Tell us what happened."

Except, we both knew what had happened.

Mr. Hughes.

"It's- it's- it's John! I knew he would be expecting me to do some-thing special on Valentine's Day so I wanted to surprise him early with s-s-" she loosed another heart-wrenching sob.

Eventually, we got it out of her.

Lyndsay told us how she'd slipped into his office between

periods and scattered rose petals all over the room. She'd put on special red lace lingerie that she'd bought just for the occasion and she was inspecting her reflection, making sure her cleavage was just so, when she heard footsteps getting closer.

Lyndsay hurriedly got into position. She reclined seductively on the desk and bit the knuckle of her middle finger to keep from laughing. It came with the added bonus of making her look extra naughty.

And then, Mr. Hughes came into his office.

And he came towing a giggling sophomore behind him.

When she saw them, Lyndsay bit into her knuckle so hard that she drew blood.

It was the only thing that kept her from screaming.

Sometimes, I think it's supposed to make somebody feel better to get something out. They force themselves to say what's wrong out loud and once they've put it out into the world, they realize it's not as awful as they thought it was in their head.

The telling only made the reality worse for Lyndsay. She was sobbing when she started telling us what happened. When she was done, she was crying so hard that she wasn't breathing. Her body couldn't take in air through the howling gasps it still needed to get out. I held her to my shoulder while Alicia continued to stroke her back. "Lyndsay, he's the one who fucked up. You deserve so much better. You really do." Alicia wasn't gloating anymore, but she still sounded like she was reading off cue cards. I just held her to me until, finally, she started to breathe normally again. By the time she wiped her nose and pulled back from me, my shoulder was soaked with her tears.

She moved to the mirror. I was watching the way she walked. Her legs were steadying. She was starting to pull herself together. Good. I didn't think her relationship with Mr. Hughes had been anything but sex. If she was calming down, then maybe she was remembering that too.

"Whatever," Lyndsay said. "I can't keep crying." She was looking at her reflection, trying to compose herself. I was relieved. Standing that close to the pit of her grief made me shiver. It felt like there were things inside of it just waiting to pull you in. "Can one of you walk with me to Principal Vernon's office?"

"...Why?" Alicia asked anxiously.

"Are you serious?!" The mad gleam in her eyes was bad in the mirror. It was worse when she turned around and let us see it straight on. "I'm going to tell him that his asshole science teacher takes blow jobs for extra credit!"

Alicia and I were both silent. But I know we were thinking the same thing.

We were thinking about the poster for the Race to Rock at the Prom that was hanging up on the wall behind her. This one had been put by the administration as propaganda. An attempt to leverage the student body's love of unjustified angsty music to get them to sit down and behave.

The poster that read, "You win when the school wins!"

"I can't believe I'm hearing this," Lyndsay said after Alicia tried to gently and carefully explain why it might not be the best idea to tell the principal what Mr. Hughes had been doing.

"Lyndsay-" Alicia tried to say.

"Especially from you with all your self-righteous bullshit!"

Alicia recoiled like she'd been burned. And, really, she had been.

"Lyndsay." At least she let me talk. "No one wants to see Mr. Hughes get what he has coming more than I do. But MVC isn't going to go anywhere near us if we turn into one of those scandal schools."

"So what?!" She grabbed at her own hair and yanked it back from her face so it hung in crazy clumps. "So I don't get some band to play at a prom I don't even want to go to anymore?!"

Neither of us had an answer for that. We didn't have anything to say about the disgust she clearly had for us either. She shook her head.

"Both of you just stay out of my way. I have to go."

She left. I turned to Alicia.

"Let me talk to her alone."

Alicia nodded. Partly because she thought maybe I could reach her and partly because she had a bathroom to herself and she certainty couldn't leave that burger and plate of fries to actually digest in her stomach.

I caught up with Lyndsay halfway down the hall.

"Lyndsay!"

She turned around.

"If you want to talk about that fucking contest again..." she warned.

"I don't," I said. "I just want you to tell me why you're doing this."

"I have to tell you?!" she shrieked.

"I helped you get ready for your first date when we were twelve," I reminded her. "I've been there for every relationship you've ever had, the good ones and the trainwrecks, and I've never seen you get this upset over a guy."

"He cheated on me!"

"So did Vin Furnier sophomore year. You were pissed for a week. Not sad, *pissed*, and then you didn't care."

"What does it matter?" She was withdrawing from me. She wanted to stay safely wrapped in her storm of unthinking anger. She didn't want to face whatever I was digging at.

But if she really wanted to leave, she could have.

"It matters because I have NEVER seen you this angry at a guy and I want to know why."

Lyndsay shuffled awkwardly. She couldn't look me in the eye.

"...And I think you ought to say it out loud," I said. I had no idea what she was actually thinking, but I didn't have to. It was obvious that she already knew. She just needed someone to force her to say it.

Lyndsay hesitated for another beat. Bracing herself for the pain that would come with bringing up whatever it was she was about to say.

"....Because I loved him."

God, really?

Fortunately, she started to sob again, scrunching her eyes shut and filling them with tears before she could see the look on my face.

"I loved him. And he hurt me."

Her tears were quiet and less hysterical, but somehow more painful. She was weeping from a wound deeper than any I could ever carve.

All because of some idiot fling she'd forget about as soon as a better set of abs walked by.

I hugged her anyway because it was clear she desperately needed one. It was also obviously the best way to keep her from doing something else stupid and torpedoing the whole school. Lyndsay slumped into my arms. I held up all of her weight and waited for her to have nothing left to cry.

"Will you do something for me?" I asked her after she was quiet again.

What?" Her words were muffled because she refused to lift herself out of my shoulder.

"Sleep on this for a night. If you still want to talk to Vernon tomorrow, I'll walk you there myself."

There was a long pause. Then, a deep sigh.

"Okay," she finally said.

"Okay," I squeezed her a little tighter just in case she changed her mind. "And think about what you want for yourself, not what you want to happen to Mr. Hughes. One way or another, I promise you that he's going to get what he has coming."

I said it without even thinking about it. I guess the things in the dark of my mental cellar had known what I needed to do the second Lyndsay broke down in tears.

Mr. Hughes was going to get what he had coming and I was going to deliver it to him personally.

One way.

And another.

Maybe a third, if he didn't lose too much blood first.

21

It's not that I don't like sex.

Really, it's not. I enjoy it when I get it. Most of the time I even let my partner live to brag about "tapping that." It never bothered me that some guys (and girls) only thought of me as breasts, legs, and ass.

They were never anything but parts to me either.

It's just that I don't understand why people get so fixated on it. The need for sex is just a basic urge like hunger or thirst; satisfy it and get on with your life. If you make it worth any more than that, you wind up like Pat Raimi, trying to babysit a lump of warm coma. Or you wind up like my parents, tethered for life to someone you can't stand.

Or, you wind up like Lyndsay.

I'd dropped Lyndsay off there often enough to know where Mr. Hughes lived. I got to his house around sunset, parked around the corner (I made sure it wasn't a permit block. I was planning to be there awhile), and waited in the bushes beside his driveway for the right opportunity.

I don't know if I was there for twenty minutes or two hours. When I'm waiting to strike there's no such thing as time. There's no such thing as texts, facebook, hunger, thirst, or sex. There's only that fixed point in time and space where I know, if I wait long enough, there's going to be blood.

The only thing I can say for sure is that it was full dark by the time Mr. Hughes came out his side door with a bag of trash. I waited until he moved free of the motion lights by his door and then I joined him in the shadows beside his garage.

"Mr. Hughes."

He jumped.

"Who's there?"

"It's just me. Beverly." I stepped out so he could see my outline if not my face. I had the porch light to my back. To him, I must have looked like nothing but darkness.

"I don't know if you recognize me, but I'm in your first period chem class."

He looked at me warily. "I know who you are. You're friends with Lyndsay."

A connection that clearly didn't thrill him.

I giggled emptily. "You don't have to worry about Lyndsay. She's fine."

"....She is?"

I laughed again. He didn't look so wary anymore. I was just a shadowy outline, but I was a very curvy outline.

"Mhm," I said. "She just wanted me to give you this." I held out a folded-up piece of paper. Mr. Hughes reached for it, but I pulled it out of reach at the last second.

"And I wanted to give you this."

I stepped against him and planted a deep, crotch-burning kiss right on his lips. I had rubbed tropical scented lotion over my neck and shoulders before going out. The scent of it must have been perfumed smoke in his nose while my lips scorched his. Mr. Hughes moaned into the kiss and tried to get his hands on my ass.

And then I too stepped just out of reach. I held the paper out to him again.

"Read this first."

He took it without a second thought, forgetting everything he'd taught children about taking things from strangers. Of course, the man liked to hook up with teenagers. I'm sure more than a couple of his "relationships" had begun with passed notes.

Though, I doubt that any of those notes said, "**Scream and I'll kill you right now.**"

I also doubt that any of his other girlfriends ever pressed the open points of a pair of industrial shears to his jugular either.

But, that's why you're not supposed to take things from strangers.

22

THE PHONE WOULD HAVE BEEN RINGING in the empty office.

Eventually, there would be a loud beep and the answering machine would kick in.

If anyone had been in the office, this is what they would have heard:

"This is John Hughes. I understand that this is very sudden but I need to take a leave of absence. There's been a family emergency back in Chicago."

I had Mr. Hughes duct taped to a chair in his kitchen. Arms, wrists, chest, ankles, knees. He was completely immobilized except for his neck. I left that free so he could wedge the phone into the cradle of his shoulder.

I was in the same room while he made his call to the office, but I wasn't exactly looming over him, ready to snatch the phone away if he tried to signal for help. When we first came into the kitchen, I'd told him I was going to duct tape him to the chair and I told him what to say and I told him what I would do if he didn't cooperate.

At first, he was skeptical of what I was saying. He thought the little blonde girl was just talking tough and playing a prank on the mean boy who dumped her little friend.

So, I put the snippety-snip mouth of the shears between his legs and I asked him if he wanted *them* to have a say in the conversation.

He took my word just fine after that.

Now, all I had to do was perch on his counter and admire the leather gloves I'd borrowed from my mother for this particular night out. I kept an ear on the conversation as I waited for him to finish. "Again, I understand how last minute this is, and I promise I'll call back with a better explanation as soon as I can."

I hopped off of the counter and sauntered over to him. He was looking right at me as he spoke.

"I'm VERY sorry about this."

It was the last thing he said before I took the phone from him and put it back on the charger.

I hung up the phone, but I left Mr. Hughes hanging. I let him stare at my back while the silence stretched on between us.

There was a block of knives directly next to the phone base. I turned my attention to the blades.

"My mother has a set of knives like this," I told him. I still hadn't turned around.

"Beverly, please... Let's talk about this. I understand you're upset, but it's not my life I'm worried about here. It's yours. You have so much..."

I drew the long butcher knife from its slot. I heard him squeak and knew how scared he was. It was the kind of sound nobody would make on purpose.

I put the butcher knife back.

I half drew out the santoku knife.

...Put it back.

I pulled another blade. A slicing knife. Identical to the one I killed Rob Cummings with.

I unsheathed this one fully. Turned towards Mr. Hughes with it.

"NO," he screamed. He tried to jerk his way free from the seat but the duct tape held him right where he was. He wasn't strong enough to break free and he wasn't slippery enough to slip out, no matter how much he was sweating.

I just slipped the knife into my purse. I could hide it in the back of a junk drawer and my mother, five months later, would finally stop complaining about the damn thing.

Mr. Hughes realized the knife wasn't for him. He slumped in his chair, sweating and trembling.

I turned my back on him again and went back to his kitchen counter.

"Beverly, listen to me," he said as I rooted through his utensil drawer. Meat thermometer? No. Garlic press? No. "I didn't want to hurt Lyndsay."

"Yeah," I said. Can opener? Interesting, but no. "But you didn't care if you did either, did you?" All of a sudden, my hand was trembling. My search for a weapon stopped being meandering and started being desperate. I was aching for something to hurt him with.

"That's not true. Lyndsay's an amazing girl."

"So what's the problem?" Now my voice was quaking too.

"There wasn't any problem! We just... we were better as friends."

That was it. Something inside of me stopped trembling and just snapped. I didn't know if what I had in my hand was something worth using but I suddenly didn't care. Lightening quick, I whipped around and it turned out I had a two-pronged bbq fork. I stabbed at his face and the tines punctured his eyeballs and he screamed as, for the first time, he really understood what being hurt meant.

Not good enough, he doesn't, something inside of me decided. *He doesn't understand nearly well enough.*

"I said, what was the problem?" I pushed the tines in deeper. "Were you blinded by a fresh piece of pussy?" I'm not sure he could even understand me. He was screaming so loud and my teeth were fused in a savage snarl that I couldn't seem to break. My words must have been barely a whisper.

Mr. Hughes was still howling. There was blood mixed with white and grey streaks of eye pulp gunk running down his face and staining his shirt.

I wasn't done.

"Or maybe you can't get it up for anyone older than sixteen?"

I stabbed the fork into his crotch. More screaming. More blood. This was getting out of hand. Someone was going to hear him screaming soon. If the police found me right now, my honor roll membership wouldn't save me. My father in the Beverly Hills Police Department would mean nothing.

I twisted the fork anyway. Mr. Hughes screamed and thrashed.

"Stop! Stop! JUDAS FUCK, STOP!"

All I heard was Lyndsay sobbing against my shoulder. And then I was replaying what he said to me while I had him in the chair. Trying to dismiss it all, trying to make it sound like her agony was an accident. Like it was just something that happened. It wasn't anybody's fault really.

I pushed the fork in deeper. "You think this hurts?!" I howled. Deeper still. I heard something pop. "How do you think Lyndsay felt after you ripped her to shreds!?!"

His face was pale as moisturizing cream. He was graying out into shock. I left the fork where it was and slapped him hard across the face.

"We're not done!" I screamed. I gave the fork another twist, really ravaging anything he had left between his legs and eliciting a fresh scream.

His screams didn't even carry half of the pain I heard in Lyndsay's cries. That's what got me, he was howling so much and he wasn't hurting nearly as bad as she was. But he was going to be. I was going to see to that. "We're just getting started, you and me," I hissed. "We're not done until I.... I..."

"I'M SORRY I'M SICK!"

I stopped. Not because of what he screamed, but because I finally realized what had been pounding in my veins ever since my hand had started to shake.

It was hate.

I stepped back from the cringing, mewling mess that was my science teacher. I was horrified.

I'd never killed out of anger. I'd never killed for hate, sorrow, or retribution.

I'd never actually wanted to kill someone before now.

I love to kill, but there's a world of difference between that and the feeling of wanting an individual person dead. I'd never felt anything but contempt for the people who were driven to kill because of their own petty, worthless "reasons." The scorned lovers, righteous fundamentalists, and pathetic rejects who decided the best way to make themselves feel important was writing their name out in blood and bullets. Death was just a tool to them. And a cheap one at that. They think they just "felt" so damn much and bloodshed was the only thing that could symbolize the unbearable weight they carried around every day.

None of them stopped to think for even a second that their "feelings" meant nothing when compared to a human life.

They made me sick.

Murder wasn't about you. It was about the victim and the act. It was about weaving yourself into the primal thread of life and death that had been first spun back at the beginning of time. To kill was to understand the savage joy that a thousand years of civilization had tried to block out and to realize just how little everything about life that wasn't death really meant.

You didn't get to throw power like that around just because you were in a pissy mood at someone.

And yet here I was, acting like some common fucking top story, troubled teen psychopath and why? Just because a guy had gotten careless with his prick? It hit me just like that. Understanding of what I was doing to Mr. Hughes washed over me in a revolting wave. The fork in my hand felt dirty. I let it drop.

Blind, Mr. Hughes had no idea why I'd relented. He was still confessing his sins to me like they could make a difference. "I can't help it. I know what I do to these girls is terrible but there's something wrong inside me. I see them and I can't stop thinking about them until they're mine. But one's never enough. It's not their fault. It's me. I'm...."

I barely heard him. I was doubled over, gritting my teeth, hooking my fingernails into my shoulders, and keeping my arms wrapped tight around my chest. I was either keeping something out or desperately trying to keep something in.

Either way, I was failing. The hatred for him was still there. I wanted the fork again. I wanted the paring knife to slip under his fingernails. I wanted the gag for his mouth so nobody would hear him scream anymore and I wanted the hot frying pan to burn shut his wounds as I went. I wanted to keep him alive for hours and then I wanted to rip his heart out, bring it to school in my purse, place it on Lyndsay's desk and say, "There. Now he knows how he made you feel."

I fell to the floor and curled up into a ball. I tried to cover my ears but the howling in my head wasn't going away.

Steve Harvey was there with it. Welcome back, Beverly. Let's start with today's categories: Things in your life worth more than torturing Mr. Hughes.

GoingtoNewYork. Killingforever. Notgoingtojail. Notlosingmymind.

Ohhhh. All good answers. But I'm sorry Beverly, this was actually a trick question. We polled a hundred chemical impulses and they're all in agreement. There is NOTHING in your life that isn't worth taking this fuckhead apart one piece at a time so you might as well go ahead and get on with it. Better luck in the next round.

No. NO. I knotted my hands into fists. No more voices. No reasoning. No bullshit. This stopped now. It stopped because I said so and I was in charge of myself. Because it was who I was and because I refused to compromise. *Because I won't be anything but who I choose to be so whatever part of me is falling apart I'm telling you to stop listening to Mr. Hughes ask for it and hold. Yourself. TOGETHER.*

I screamed the last part into my own mind. I poured every piece of willpower I had into a desperate, frantic, last stand for my soul.

And then I reached for the fork anyway.

An inch closer, and that would have been it. A concerned faculty member or the cops would have found me a day later, mauling Mr.

Hughes' corpse with my bare hands because I'd already tried every-thing else in the house that could be used as a weapon.

But the fork was just far enough away. Far enough that I had to stretch and far enough that I had the extra second I needed to get ahold of myself. My hand slapped down and felt cold tile instead of warm wood. I squeezed, trying to anchor myself into the hard linoleum like it was soil but just breaking every nail on that hand instead.

I didn't care. I didn't give a shit about the pain or how I was going to look the next day. All I cared about was that, gradually, the whirlwind that drowned out all other thoughts was fading. I waited, terrified that I might lose it again, but all I heard was my own breath heaving raggedly in the back of my throat.

Slowly, I worked my way up to my knees. My head was pounding worse than the morning after me, Lyndsay, and Alicia killed our first handle of vodka. My throat hurt too. Had I been screaming? I didn't think so but I couldn't say for sure.

In front of me, Mr. Hughes was still blubbering. About what, I had no idea.

"-I can be better. I promise. I'll get help. I'll see a shrink. Just give me a chance. Please. Please, I know I can be different."

I forced myself to pick up the fork again and stood up. I was glad Mr. Hughes couldn't see the way I was still trembling. I made my way towards him but it was all wrong. I didn't feel dangerous or gifted. I shuffled across the kitchen like the Earth could be yanked out from under me at any second. That, or I might just throw up in the sink.

"I'll quit my job. I'll move. I'll-"

I got my free hand into his mouth and grabbed his tongue. I pulled it out to the tearing point and pressed the tines of the bbq fork to it. "This is the fork you're feeling again," I said. My voice was cold and flat. Nothing angry in it. Nothing vengeful. "If you want to be even more useless to a woman, keep talking. If not, then shut your fucking mouth."

He got very quiet. I kept the points to his flesh while I waited for my arm to stop quivering. But the shakes were ok. I was back in control now and I knew I wasn't going to put a metal point through this squirmy piece of pink flesh unless I wanted to. I had to trust myself. Especially so soon after almost completely losing control; I had to trust myself or else one day I was going to wind up dead or in a padded room.

"You won't say anything about me?" I asked.

"Nothing!"

"And you'll apologize to Lyndsay?"

"As soon as I can. I want to. I want to be better."

That makes two of us. I pulled the fork away. I considered the quivering, bleeding mess in front of me. I felt better. I didn't hate this pathetic thing anymore.

"Alright."

"...Alright?"

Alright," I repeated. I sat in his lap. Wrapped my arms around his neck.

Yes, much better.

"Just learn from this, ok?" I told him. "Years from now, if you can find a girl who'll love you despite your... handicaps, just treat her right, ok?"

I kissed him on the sodden cheek and tasted the salt of his sweat and tears. I stood up. Backed out into the living room. I made sure to make plenty of noise so he would know that I was leaving. There was no way he didn't hear my footfalls across the wooden floor or the creak as I opened the front door. I know for sure he heard it when I closed the door because he collapsed in his chair and started sobbing with relief. I listened to him sniffle and wheeze and whimper.

Then, without making a single sound, I crept back into the kitchen. He was still weeping.

I smirked when he shot back up rigidly at the creak of an opening cabinet.

He looked around wildly at the sound of groaning wood as I lifted the bottle out from under the sink.

"Is someone there?!"

He was so terrified. I bit my tongue to keep from laughing. I was feeling really good now. Good enough to think up a third thing that Mr. Hughes had coming.

"Beverly? BEVERLY?!"

He was listening intently. Still blind of course. No idea what was going on. No way for him to know if I was still there or if he was just jumping at sounds of the house settling.

"....Beverly?"

"Yes, Mr. Hughes?"

I was right in front of him and he didn't even know it until I jammed the open bottle of drain cleaner into his mouth.

He tried to scream but with the bottle in his mouth I didn't have to worry about anyone else hearing it anymore. What his muted shrieks lacked in volume they made up for in sheer pain as the corrosive liquid ate its way down his throat. He tried to jerk his head from side to side but only succeeded in splashing burning patches across his lips and cheeks.

Completely sane again, I forced his head back and increased the flow of drain cleaner from the bottle. I watched Mr. Hughes foam at the mouth and convulse against the bonds that held him in the chair. The drain cleaner was bleaching his lips white, but I wanted to turn the rest of his tan face that same milky color if I could.

It never did, it turned a murky gray at best, but I watched him die with a smile. Not on Lyndsay's behalf, not because of anything he'd done wrong that I'd set right. I smiled because I was on the hunt.

And I would have my kill.

23

I ROLLED into the driveway with the car in neutral and my lights turned off. It was three o'clock and I was being careful. I didn't know if my parents knew I was out or if they even cared. They'd been giving me plenty of space since I started showing an interest in life after high school, but getting chewed out over curfew was the last thing I needed right now. My night had been bad enough as it was.

Mr. Hughes' next door neighbors didn't go to sleep until 12 o'clock. Which meant I had to wait until midnight before it was quiet enough to carry my three garbage bags full of Mr. Hughes out to the car. Then, there was an accident on the highway so it took me an hour to get to Pico-Union. Add to all of that my hand with the broken nails that still burned like an open wound dipped in vodka, and all I wanted to do was just go to sleep.

Sleep and forgetfulness. That was what I needed. As I crept upstairs, I was still chastising myself for losing control like that with Mr. Hughes. If all I wanted to be was some stupid, impulsive brat, I shouldn't even bother going east. I might as well just stay home with my....

My parents' light was still on.

"I don't know what you want me to say," I heard my dad say through the door.

"I want you to say that I'm right, Jerry!" Mom, obviously.

I stopped. I pressed my ear to the door.

"I-I...." It definitely sounded like my dad, but his voice was robbed of the absolute authority I always associated with it. He was unsure. Hesitant.

"Tina, if this is about-"

"IT'S ABOUT EVERYTHING," she exploded. But I heard no anger in her voice. Only anguish. "We're not working, Jerry. You know it and I know it so let's just... agree. I have a friend in legal who referred me to someone who does divorce work. He can have the papers drawn up by the end of the week. It'll be a straight split, everything right down the middle. You have my word on that."

Again, no anger. No desire to hurt him. Just an honest feeling I couldn't quite place.

A long beat of silence followed. Finally, my dad spoke.

"June."

"What?"

"I said June. Let's just give Beverly a proper home through graduation."

"You spoil that girl," she said. She was back to her normal, brusque tone. I had no idea how much I depended on it until she had said a single sentence in that other, quiet voice.

"That girl is our daughter," he said. Again, not angry. Not trying to score points. "And she doesn't need to deal with this when she should be enjoying her last year of high school.

Enjoy? My dad had laid out a long list of things I was supposed to achieve this year, but enjoyment was never one he mentioned to me.

"Fine," Mom said. "June first. Let's just get some sleep."

The light shut off.

I was left in the dark.

24

....My parents were getting a divorce.

I laid in my bed and tried to break it down into pieces that made sense.

Which shouldn't have been hard to do, because it made perfect sense. My parents didn't like each other. At all. Why would they possibly want to stay married? I'm sure if I'd thought about it more before now then I wouldn't even be surprised.

Besides, this was a good thing. I was wracking my brains for reasons to stay away from my life in LA and here was a perfect one dropped right in front of me. Now, when I told them I didn't want to come home for the summer, or even Christmas, they would just assume it was because of the split and that they needed to "give me my space."

It was perfect really.

I had problems getting to sleep that night, but only because of the adrenaline still running through my system after (*Torturing. Call it what it is. You tortured-*) Mr. Hughes.

It didn't make it any better that I was having trouble breathing. Last time I did anything that made me inhale that much drain cleaner fumes.

25

THE NEXT MORNING, Lyndsay wasn't there before school. We got to chemistry class early to wait by her desk but, with a minute to go before first period, she still wasn't there.

Mr. Hughes was obviously running a little behind as well.

"Have you talked to her?" Alicia asked.

"Not since yesterday."

"I wouldn't blame her for not coming in after what that prick did to her," Alicia said. *Of course,* I thought, *if she didn't come in then she also can't talk to Vernon.*

"We just have to give her time. I think she'll be okay eventually."

But Alicia wasn't looking at me anymore. She was looking over my shoulder.

"....I don't think you have to think about it."

I turned around. So did every guy in the classroom.

Lyndsay was in the doorway.

She looked amazing.

I mean, Lyndsay's naturally good looking but the girl who showed up to class was at a whole other level. Her hair was shining and windswept in that perfect California way no one can really get.

Her makeup was subtle enough to look like she was that hot without any makeup. She was dressed to show off just enough of her body to make you desperate to see the rest of it.

It was obvious now why she was late. This whole package must have taken her hours to put together. It was far too much effort to do for anything but your prom or your wedding.

But, if you just broke up with a guy and wanted to make him.... well, if you wanted to make him stab himself in the face with a fork, it might be worth it then too.

Lyndsay walked over to us. She was trying to act like she didn't notice everyone drooling after her and doing a poor job of it. Her whole face was split by an impossibly wide grin.

It was the only part of her ensemble that took five seconds to do and it was the most appealing part by far.

"Hey guys," she said.

Even Alicia and I were gawking.

"Lyndsay," Alicia said. "You look-"

"Amazing? I know."

Something struck Alicia. She looked at Lyndsay with a more skeptical eye.

"This isn't just some trick to get Mr. Hughes back is it?"

"John? Ew, no. Fuck him. Fuck him, fuck his whore, and fuck every guy who thinks they can screw around behind my back and get away with it."

And she meant it, she really did. Alicia laughed and high-fived her. Lyndsay turned towards me. I held my hand up too, why the hell not?

And then Lyndsay enveloped me in a huge hug I never saw coming.

"Oof," I grunted. She ignored me and just squeezed tighter.

But this wasn't like yesterday. This hug wasn't trying to take anything, it wasn't the drowning woman's desperate clutch.

This hug was trying to give.

"Thank you so much," she whispered in my ear. The clothes and the hair and the cleavage might have been for everyone else. Those four words were meant just for me.

But for what? Mr. Hughes was currently rat chow in the basement of an abandoned apartment building somewhere off of West Olympic Boulevard. Nobody knew he was dead yet. So what was she thanking me for? It couldn't be that load of crap I fed her at school to keep her from going to Vernon.

But she was still hugging me. There were waves of warmth coming off of her that I'd never experienced before.

"What are friends for?" I said, only because I didn't know what else to say.

The bell rang, mercifully, before I had to say anything else.

"Come on," Lyndsay said. "I want the best seat in the house when Mr. Hughes sees me and drops his stupid, oversized jaw."

We went to our seats. Lyndsay tossed her hair back and sat up just so. She didn't bother to ask me if I thought she looked good.

And then a woman entered. An older, soft around the middle, obviously did her own hair coloring, woman.

"Good morning, class," she said. "My name is Mrs. Baker. Mr. Hughes had to be called away for a family emergency so I'll be teaching his class until he returns. Now, if you're all ready to begin..."

She went to his desk for the attendance book.

The rumors started to fly as soon as class let out. They'd been building for years and his sudden "absence" was the clap that started the avalanche. For the rest of the day, you could hear lots of "Dude, Mr. Hughes...."

"He was-"

"....She was going to tell so he-"

By the time I got to my locker at the end of the day, there were also rumors that he was dealing steroids to the junior varsity football team, having an affair with Coach Shipman, and left school to start a career in porn.

So long as nobody started talking about him getting hacked up by a beautiful blonde, it all seemed like good fun to me. Maybe I'd make up my own version.

Anthony was by the lockers. He was actually looking at me for once.

I smiled. "Hey, boyfriend."

26

ANTHONY

I TOTALLY HAD things I was going to say.

I had a plan in my head to get me through this whole conversation. Pre-planned jokes. Prepared questions. Various alternate conversation flowcharts to account for anything she might say.

And then she went ahead and called me "boyfriend" and my brain stopped functioning. It just cold stopped working while Beverly stood there and waited for me to do something except stand there and gape like an idiot.

"Hello," you moron. Is "Hello" too freaking hard to get out?

Apparently, it was.

You could just go for "hi."

Nope, not happening.

And then my phone beeped in my pocket.

"Heh, one second," I squeaked and took it out. Jesus, now I was ignoring her. Then again, don't girls like it when guys act like jerks? *They like it when the guy's good looking. Not when he should be grateful he's even in the same zip code.*

It was a text from Curtis:

"Beverly, do you want to practice our lines this weekend?"

I looked up. Curtis was down the hall, waving furiously at me and making the universal gesture for, "Get on with it you fucking pussy."

I pocketed my phone. Turned back to Beverly.

"Sorry," I said.

"That's ok," she said. She was so sweet.

"Anyway, I was thinking maybe before rehearsal starts we could get together and run some of our lines? You know, get a head start before Alicia motivates us with a heel in the ass."

Oh God, I'd just insulted her friend.

But she was laughing before I could panic and shut down again.

"That sounds like an idea," she said. "Alicia's been on a Gucci kick lately. Those things are monsters." She grabbed a pen. Then she grabbed my hand.

SHE GRABBED MY HAND.

"This is my address...." She wrote on my palm. "Saturday at three?"

There was no way I could talk. I nodded.

She smiled. "Great, see you then."

I bit my tongue to keep from grinning like a complete idiot. As is, I still did a smile-nod like a tourist who can't speak English and stumbled around the corner.

When I was mercifully out of sight, I collapsed against a wall of lockers and let out a shaky breath.

I couldn't stop trembling. I had a feeling that I now knew what it was like to be in the middle of a firefight. When it's going on, it's all life or death decisions with no margin for error and so much frantic activity that you don't even know your own name.

Then, when it's over, the reality of what just happened hits you like a hammer all at once and you have a seizure.

But, terrifying or not, I had her address on my palm.

I was going to encase my hand in Lucite.

27

"So, while you could barely get a word out, guess who was dropping some rock solid game."

I tucked the bluetooth headset more securely into my ear. "What the hell are you talking about?"

"I'm talking about the parking lot, man. I'm talking about walking to my car, debating whether to go Taco Bell or In 'n Out-"

"In 'n Out. That's never even a discussion."

"You're right, it's not. But that's when I hear Lyndsay Coleman, and you know how hot she looked yesterday, start screaming out, 'Oh no! Oh, shit!'

"So, I look around and she's next to her car, looking into the window, jiggling the door handle, stomping around in circles, and then repeating the whole dance like something different's going to happen.

"Nobody else is doing anything so I go over. I mean, what the fuck right? If you're anything to go by, the universal laws of hot chicks and freaks have gone totally backwards. And I ask her what's wrong and she says, 'I lost my keys.'

So then I say, 'You lost your keys?' because the second I opened my mouth I was suddenly completely terrified and all I could do was act like a damn parrot."

"Not so easy is it?"

"Nope. But anyway, she just laughs and goes, 'I know. Blonde, right?' She holds up her hair to show me, like there's anything about her I'm not completely aware of. And then she says that of course it's the one day she forgot her phone and she asks if she can borrow mine. I'm digging it out to give it to her when she starts looking at me weird. And then she asks me if we've met before. I didn't want to get into the whole thing but I tell her, 'Yeah, our moms are friends and we used to hang out sometimes when we were five or, you know, ten."

"Is that true?"

"Dude, hand to God. I spent every New Years Eve, Halloween, and Fourth of July with that girl until she got old enough to not want to be anywhere near her mother anymore. And here's the thing, when I reminded her, her eyes got HUGE. She totally remembered me. And before puberty hit me and ran without leaving a note, I was actually pretty adorable."

I was doubtful, but I let him have his moment.

"And that's when I get to thinking, maybe she doesn't even need her phone. So, I run over real quick to the tennis court-"

I groaned. "You didn't."

"-I come back with a tennis ball and a pen, you fucking skeptic. I poke a hole in the ball, press the hole over the lock, smack the ball with my fist and punch out a blast of air, and... this is why you shouldn't doubt YouTube, asshole."

"So what happened then? Did you whisk her off in your Camaro for two point five minutes of odd squelching noises?"

"No, but after I got the door open, she was looking at me, man."

"Looking at you weird?"

"No, I mean looking at me REALLY weird."

I laughed. "Well, I'm almost at Beverly's now. I'll ask if Lyndsay does any activities in the Spring we could get you involved in. Though if she does anything physical I think you're out of luck."

"Anthony, for that girl I'd train to run a marathon."

"And I'd start working out things to say for your eulogy."

"Start with my good looks."

I was pulling up to Beverly's house. "I don't know if a funeral's an appropriate venue to start off with a joke. Listen, man. I've got to go."

"Say no more. Godspeed, Brotha."

I hung up.

Talking to Curtis on the drive over had been a nice distraction. I know you're not supposed to drive and talk on the phone, but if I hadn't been I probably would've crashed just out of sheer nerves.

I kept that momentum going by walking fast to the door. That was the key, keep moving forward, don't give yourself time to think about what you're doing and shit yourself.

I rang the bell and prayed, *pleaseanswerbeforeIcanthink, pleaseanswerbeforeIcanthink.*

She did. God, she looked beautiful.

"Hey, Anthony!"

"Hey," my voice didn't even waver. I was getting good at this.

Then she air-kissed me on the cheek and I nearly collapsed on the floor.

No. No. You are normal. You are going to be fucking normal.

So, holding my legs up by sheer force of will, I walked into the house.

And I tripped over the doorframe on my way in.

"Whoops," Beverly giggled. "You ok?"

No. Probably never by this point. Desperate for something to say, I looked around the living room. "Wow, nice house."

"Thanks. We used the same home designer as the Kardashians."

"I don't know if I'd brag about that." I wasn't dumb enough to say that loudly. I was just mumbling to myself, still trying to get back my composure, but she must have fantastic hearing to go with everything else because she laughed and shrugged. Still, she laughed so... win?

"Is down here ok?" she asked, indicating the living room. "Or do you wanna go up to my room? It's quieter there."

Don't say her room, I told myself. *Her room is the creep answer. You might as well suggest she do the scene in her underwear.*

Of course, I'd already said "your room," the second she'd offered.

But, hopefully not in a creepy way.

I walked up the stairs side by side with her so she wouldn't think I was looking at her ass as she walked.

That should count for something.

28

"LOST IN THE CHURN."

"Lost in the churn!"

God was I ever. My brain was butter the second I walked into her room. I was trying to absorb every square inch of wallpaper while still carrying on a conversation and rehearsing a musical number.

I said it from the beginning, I didn't just lust after Beverly Kilbourne, I loved her. I wanted to know everything about who she really was.

I wanted to know the Beverly nobody else did.

OK, her room wasn't exactly the Fortress of Solitude, but I wondered how many people knew she had a collection of Mexican folk-art skeletons. Or if anybody else had noticed the small stack of Raymond Chandler and Brett Easton Ellis novels tucked in a corner by her bed.

"Nowhere to turn."

"Nowhere to turn!"

Every treasure like that I uncovered, every stupid thing I saw like an errant disc from a film noir DVD set, I forgot more of the fictional Beverly I'd created over the last three years and fell more deeply in love with the real Beverly I was coming to know.

We fell in together for the next part, looked each other in the eye as if we were performing for a crowd of hundreds:

"I don't know what to do without you

I don't know who I'd be

If I didn't have yoouuuu"

The last note faded. I waited expectantly for Beverly to take over.

She looked back at me. I forgot what we were supposed to be doing, mesmerized by her glinting blue eyes. I abandoned everything else willingly. Anything and everything, so long as I could stay in the thrall of those eyes.

And then she realized she'd missed her cue and broke eye contact. My consolation prize was the sight of her collapsing on her bed in a fit of laughter.

"I'm sorry. I'm sorry," she said between bouts of laughter. I'd overheard her laughing with her friends before. Actually being in on the joke was the difference between listening to a recorded track and being in the front row at an intimate concert venue.

"It's ok," I said. "We've only gone through this five times."

"It's hard," she protested. She pretended to be upset. Her faux frown turned her mouth into the most perfect little bow.

In spite of this, I realized we were having a normal conversation. I wasn't blushing or forgetting how to talk. I was becoming comfortable with her.

"It's musical theatre," I told her. "It can't be hard. It's literally acting for people not good enough to be in movies and singers not good enough to get record deals," I joked. An actual, unplanned, not driven by fear joke. "The whole thing's built on not being hard."

"If theatre's so dumb, how come you auditioned?"

Ah, there was the blushing and inability to speak. Good to have you back.

I struggled to vamp (that's a showbiz term). "Well... you know...

It's senior year. I haven't done any extracurricular stuff people actually care about..."

"It's ok, Anthony," she said. "I think I know what you're doing."

"Y-you do?"

Had I been that obvious? I hadn't meant to be.

She nodded. She didn't look grossed out or like she was trying to let me down gently. She was smiling just a little. The kind of little where maybe someone was trying hard not to smile a lot. "Mhm. And I think it's a pretty cool way to put yourself out there."

Ok, what the actual hell? What the hell do I do with this? Is she actually flirting with me? Was there a subtext in the invitation to her room that I missed? Does she want me to try and kiss her? If I wait, is she going to kiss me?

I had no idea. I just knew that if I made a move and Beverly didn't want me to, then it would be a disaster. I looked to her body language for some kind of clue, but there was still only that thin, miniscule hint of a smile.

It was the single best smile I'd ever seen in my entire life but I had no idea where it was trying to lead me.

"Do you....Do you think it's working?" I needed more information but what if that was the wrong thing to say? This was nerve-wracking. I had no idea how anybody did this all the time.

Her smile widened. Just a little. She looked me right in the eye.

"I think it might be," she said.

But she stayed standing where she was. She didn't make any attempt to close the distance between us.

I was starting to get the message. She knew what I was doing, and she was possibly coming around to the idea, but I couldn't pressure her. I certainly wasn't supposed to make a move right now. But, if I gave her time, then maybe she would. I just had to wait a little longer.

And that was okay. It wasn't like I wasn't already waiting for her.

Also, I was wrong. *This* was as good as it got. It had to be. If by the end of the year I actually kissed Beverly Kilbourne then I was going to start thinking that I'd been hit by a car before the audition and all of this was an elaborate hallucination as I spent my final minutes bleeding out in the school parking lot.

"You want to go through the song again?" I asked. Though I wasn't going to make a particularly good tormented, dying artist if I couldn't stop grinning like I got a dose of Joker gas.

But Beverly shook her head.

"It's getting late and I'm meeting some people later. But this was fun. Let's make it a thing."

A thing.

Beverly Kilbourne and I had a thing.

I didn't walk down the steps, I slid down the banister. I danced across the living room.

I opened the door and came face to face with her father. Her father who was always the cop who came to career day.

I stopped dancing. Came to a jerking stop a second before I would have bowled him over.

"Oh, jeez. Sorry, sir."

He didn't seem particularly bothered. With the daughter he had, and the Beverly Hills PD marksmanship awards he boasted about every career day, I'm sure he was used to meeting flustered, terrified boys.

"That's alright."

He stuck out his hand.

"I'm Beverly's father."

I shook his hand. He squeezed pretty hard but I think I held up alright. "Anthony Kilmeade. Pleasure to meet you, sir."

"Pleasure's all mine, son." I don't think I believed it. There was something in his eyes that told me he used that same voice to call people "son" if they looked like they were casing a jewelry store.

"Well, have a good night," I said. I let him enter, doing my best to seem extra courteous, and then I was gone. I felt his gaze on my back the whole way to the car but, short of feeling a bullet instead, nothing could dim the elation I felt.

29

BEVERLY

I CAME DOWN the stairs not long after Anthony left. I'd already dressed before he came over and all I had to do now was tie my hair back, throw my ID and my mom's meat tenderizer in my purse, and I was good to go.

I told Anthony I was meeting people, and that was true. But who I was meeting was still up in the air. I could cruise behind the restaurants in Los Feliz and pick off two or three writer/busboys taking out the trash. Or, if I was in the mood for quality over quantity, I could go to Silverlake and drink two dollar PBRs until some guy in a Fedora decided that he was more interested in great breasts than he was in whether or not they came packaged in a post-ironic t-shirt.

I blamed the musical. Ever since we started rehearsing, I'd been craving hipsters.

And it didn't have to be a male hipster. It just so happened that it was usually easier for me to lure in guys than girls but, when it came to murder, I was totally bi-merciless.

My dad was in the foyer when I came down the stairs. He saw me coming and I waved noncommittally. "Later, dad."

"I just ran into a friend of yours. Who's Anthony?"

"He's playing my boyfriend in the show."

"Just playing?" he asked slyly.

I rolled my eyes. "Yes, daddy. Just playing."

"Shame," he said. "I liked him. He seemed polite."

"He's also gay."

"Really?" he asked doubtfully. "That one?"

Well, at least I knew where my shoddy gaydar came from.

"Yes, that one. The guy playing his best friend is gay too. Anthony just auditioned because he's this shy little nobody who'd never talk to him otherwise." At least, that's the narrative Alicia and I came up with. It was the only story that made sense.

My dad walked over to the liquor cabinet. "Well, if he's playing your boyfriend then he's also got a lot of scenes with you. Who knows, maybe you can fix him."

"Daddy!"

He waved his drink disdainfully. "I'm old and insensitive. Fine."

I shook my head. "I'll see you later, dad."

"Beverly."

I stopped with my hand on the door. I turned but my dad still had his back to me. His head was turned down to his drink.

I don't know about insensitive, but he looked very old.

"Your mother and I love you," he said. "You know that, don't you?"

"I know."

"Good. That's.... that's important."

No, it wasn't.

It was nothing. Less than nothing. It was the first piece of dead weight I wanted to leave in the Pacific Time Zone.

But, that wasn't the question he asked me. He just asked me if I knew that their love for me existed.

I did; and there was no reason for me to say anything else.

INTERLUDE FOUR:

APRIL

Ken McCammon lived with nothing for a very long time.

Growing up, he had nothing. Going out on his own as a high school dropout, he had nothing. After living in a van and migrating through the Venice Beach area for twenty years he had... he had a van and an admirable collection of ZZ Top bumper stickers but not much else.

So, when he became a viral sensation after taking part in a local news interview while soaring on 2 tabs of acid and a gallon of Colt .45, it's understandable how his financial planning skills might leave something to be desired.

When the royalty checks for the t-shirts, rap remixes, and the print ad for Colt .45 started coming in, the first thing he did was sign a one-year lease on a house in Marina Del Rey. The second thing he did was install a freezer in every room and stock each one with as much Johnny Walker Blue as he could fit.

After that came the boat. Then the car. Then the skybox at the Staples Center. He only wanted it for the ZZ Top show in August, but you never knew who might come to town.

Ken could not possibly have the sustained income to support all of these things. If ZZ Top is in Los Angeles again this time next year, Ken likely won't be able to afford the parking at the Staples Center.

But, that is a problem for later and Ken has never worried too much about later.

Right now, the money is pouring in and Ken is sprawled out on the front row couch in his private theatre. The lights are down and the MVC music block is on the TV. They never play the good stuff like they did when Ken was growing up but he still has a soft spot for the network.

Also, that Linea Q babe who introduces the videos is so fucking hot.

"Hey guys," Linea says to the camera. "Like the hair?" She points to her orange and black hair, different from last week's blue and green. "I know it's not halloween, but I had to do it because I was SO impressed when I heard about what they were doing down at John Carpenter High in California. We've got Damien in Century City right now with the details."

The camera cuts away to a high school gymnasium and a male correspondent. Twenty-five at best and dressed by committee to appear as edgy as possible while still sporting at least three designer tags. Next to him is a high school senior. Six feet and a hundred and eighty pounds of privilege and stupidity.

"Hey, Linea," Damien says. "I'm here with Gunnar Hewitt who's gonna tell us a little about what he did for his friend, Rob."

Damien hands the mic over. Gunnar takes it and flashes the camera an oozing, solicitous smile.

"So yeah, basically my friend Rob was murdered in September." His smile fades but it never really goes away. "And a bunch of us wanted to, you know, honor him."

As the interview goes on, the silhouette of a woman appears at the back of the theatre with a bottle of scotch. She doesn't move to snuggle back beside Ken on the couch yet, her shadow merely leans in the doorway. She watches the monologue on screen with barely suppressed amusement.

"Every year we have this fundraiser for prom so, for this year's theme, we decided to collect the money in Rob's honor and make him our honorary prom king." He taps his chest and points at the camera with two fingers.

"Love you, bro. Miss ya every day."

The woman with the bottle steps forward. She's unscrewing the bottle cap but she's walking past Ken and towards the screen. Her shadow blocks Ken's view of Linea Q but the view of the girl's tight outline in Yoga pants makes it hard to complain.

The camera cuts back to the studio.

"For this touching memorial," Linea says, treating the idea of a murdered teenager with the same praise as a successful carwash, "We're giving John Carpenter High fifty big points."

The shadow woman sprays a fan of scotch across the screen.

Ken doesn't object. Not at the stains on his projector screen and not at the trail of two hundred dollar scotch she's splashing between the screen and his couch.

This could be because the girl he brought home is so beautiful, so impossibly sexual, that she can do whatever she wants so long as she doesn't leave.

Or, it might be because Beverly's already slit his throat.

In the light of the projector screen, she's no longer a shadow. At least, not on the outside. She looks down on Ken's body. She sees the shock and horror still frozen on his face and thinks, minus the bloody gorge across his throat, that Alicia must have the same look on her face as she hears Linea Q say, "And with only a month to go, that gives them a thirty five point lead and makes them the odds on favorite to win the MVC Race to Rock at the Prom!"

Linea keeps talking but Beverly no longer hears it. She's impatiently watching the dark stream of scotch bend and curve down the dead man's face. She needs the body to be soaked before she can continue, but the waiting is so impossibly hard.

Soon, the book of matches in her hip pocket promises. *Soon.*

To hell with soon.

The bottle's not done but she drops it in his lap regardless. She takes out the matches. The first love she's never quite gotten over.

She strikes one and sets it to the rest of the match heads in the book. The whole packet goes up in her hand. She feels everything that she is, her desires, her hope, her passion, all dancing hungrily within the power flickering at her fingertips.

She tosses the bundle of destruction at Ken's chest. The fire ignites the scotch soaked fabric and soon his entire face and torso is burning merrily. A moment later, the trail from the floor to the screen catches and the inferno that will consume the house and everything in it has begun.

Beverly watches for longer than she should. If she's not quick, someone might see her leaving the burning house, but she can't help herself.

The fire always has that effect on her.

Behind her, Linea Q is still going through her spiel, oblivious to the flames licking at her cheery visage.

"Now, pop quiz for you guys at home. What does this new single from Everything's Eventual and our Race to Rock at the Prom Contest have in common? They're both heating up!"

The bad pun brings her back to reality. Beverly still hasn't seen enough, but she's able to pull herself away from the fire.

30

BEVERLY

BY REHEARSAL THE NEXT DAY, Alicia's reaction had moved past the "shock and horror" phase in favor of the phase where she wanted to do the throat cutting herself.

I was the last person into the auditorium. The rest of the cast was already there and stage crew was hard at work setting up the "shitty apartment" set.

"Beverly!"

That was Clay. Even if I hadn't heard him, it'd be impossible to miss him running at me. His hair was bleached white blonde and he was always dressed in bright pastels and glaring patterns. He'd moved here from rural Texas two years ago and his wardrobe and mannerisms showed it. Everything about him was fifteen years of quietly building "I'M GAY" exploding in a blinding, atom bomb glare.

He kissed me on each cheek. "You're late," he told me.

"Rehearsal's not til four."

"Oh, you're fine for rehearsal." He took me by the arm and led me towards the stage. "It's our PMS-ing fearless leader I could use your help with. With opening night so close, she's turning into a real drama queen."

Alicia didn't look up from her notebook. "Clay, the only queen I see here is you. Now shut your mouth and get on stage with Anthony."

Clay's jaw dropped comically. He pressed an offended hand to his chest and reared back in a parody of outrage.

I smirked as he sashayed onto the stage. I was starting to get a real soft spot for him and Anthony. The two of them reminded me of adorable little kittens. If Anthony ever got his nerve up enough to ask Clay out, I hoped they'd have fun together.

I took my seat next to Alicia. "Ouch," I murmured to her.

"I'm in a bad mood," she said by way of a justification if not an apology. "Did you see the MVC news last night?"

I shrugged. "I caught it."

"Then you saw that memorial bullshit JCH is pulling."

"That's a little harsh."

"All year and they don't even plant a tree for the moron," she persisted. "Now that there's a month left in the contest, they decide it's a good time to hold a memorial baseball game for the *football* captain."

"Molly's still got that big dent in her skull," I joked. "Maybe we could donate the proceeds from the play to some kind of head injury rehabilitation center."

"No good," Alicia said, completely serious. ""She's a pretty white girl and she's still alive. If we really wanted some sympathy votes, we'd need someone to commit a hate crime on school grounds or something."

She got up and went over to the stage to coach Clay and Anthony.

I stayed where I was and thought about hate crimes and sympathy.

I thought about kittens and how appalled people would be at the thought of someone crushing their little kitty skulls.

I looked at Clay and Anthony and thought about what I could do to make the wound left by the six-month-old passing of a mediocre football talent look like a paper cut.

On stage, Anthony caught me looking at him and waved hesitantly.

"Anthony! Eyes front!"

Chastised, he turned back to Alicia but kept sneaking looks at me.

Eyes glinting, I waved back at him.

If Anthony was going to make a move, he'd better make it soon.

31

IT WASN'T EASY, but I starved myself for three weeks.

No knives. No hammers. No frat boys. No party girls. *Nothing.* I couldn't ensure the whole city of Los Angeles would be on its best behavior, but I could do my part to look extra typical for a couple weeks.

It was torture. I had a countdown programed into my phone and there were nights where I swear it was running backwards.

Alicia saw that countdown once. She got really excited that I had a countdown to the play on my phone.

I never bothered to tell her what I was really counting down to.

Even if it felt like a hundred years later, eventually the opening night of the show was upon us. Alicia had us all there prepping at five and by six thirty the auditorium was already filling with friends, family, amateur theatre lovers, and professional lovers of Beverly Kilbourne in a tube top and hotpants.

To quote Alicia, whatever put asses in the seats.

Speaking of Alicia, the Head Bitch herself was backstage dishing out last minute orders to a dozen departments.

"Move that bed closer to center stage! Make sure the first song's cued up! I need two people back here to prep those trash cans, I don't care what department they're in!"

She kept going, hurling orders in every direction. All of this had been planned out differently with the department chairs weeks ago but it didn't matter. Alicia was operating from her gut now, that place of last minute, instinctive brilliance that said, "Hey! Forget the screwdriver you brought with you and do something inventive with a pineapple corer instead!"

It made me feel bad for her. All this work and the curtain was never going to even come up.

I felt bad for me too. It turned out that I enjoyed acting. Not enough to make a career out of it, but I enjoyed how the craft was like turning yourself into a mirror ball. It wasn't really pretending to be someone else, it was more like just rotating your soul to change the reflection that people could see.

I consoled myself by remembering that once I got to New York I could be an acting major if I wanted to. In a lot of ways it was actually perfect. It was an excuse to be a waitress or something menial forever and it was a justification to stay in New York through the summer. All I had to do was tell my parents that theatre was my passion and I didn't care if I ever made a cent off of it, acting was an expression of who I really was and nothing else would ever make me happy.

I wouldn't have to even work that hard to make it sound convincing. The only lie would be the part about acting.

A large spotlight suddenly shone down on Alicia. She grimaced and covered her eyes against the blinding glare. "Jesus, Curtis. Cut that by half."

By the lighting controls, Curtis winced. "Sorry," he said. He fiddled with the controls but Alicia was already moving on to yell at somebody else. "God damn miserable bitch," he muttered when she was very safely out of earshot. I heard him but I certainly wasn't going to tell her. Alicia would kill him.

"Hi!" The voice came from behind both Curtis and I. He jumped. I didn't.

Not that anyone cared. Lyndsay hadn't even noticed me. She was too busy giggling at Curtis as he whirled around in alarm.

"Sorry," she said in a voice that made it clear how not sorry she really was.

"Don't mention it," Curtis said. He was still panting. "Just let me find the kidney you made me shit out."

She laughed. This time with him, not at him.

No way. She isn't.

"I didn't know you were stage crew," she said.

"That's because I'm usually not. Anthony roped me into helping."

Oh my God, she is.

"I know what you mean. Alicia's got me handing out fliers." She mimed putting a gun to her head and pulled the thumb trigger. "Buutttt," she went on, "I handed out all my fliers so now I'm just hanging."

"You want to help me?"

"Okay."

Curtis was joking but no stage light in the world could have lit up as brightly as he did when he realized that Lyndsay was dead serious. And she was. All of the classic signs were there. The one knee bent slightly in his direction, twirling her hair as she talked to him. She was going deep.

They still hadn't noticed me. Nobody had. That rarely happened in general. It never happened when I was three quarters undressed. A happy collision of puppy love and fear of Alicia.

I took the opportunity and slipped into the hallway.

I was heading for the dressing rooms.

I ran into Clay first.

"Heyyyy, Beverly."

We embraced. Exchanged cheek kisses.

"Look at you," he crowed. "You look better in those shorts than I would!"

I laughed, but I was also scanning the hallway around us. No good. Too many witnesses scurrying back and forth doing Alicia's bidding.

"You can borrow them after the show," I told him.

"Please, maybe if I lost five pounds."

We both laughed.

"Where's Anthony?" I asked.

"His dressing room," Clay said. "I was just about to go get him."

"Oh, I'll get him," I said. "Go on stage. You're gonna knock 'em dead, Clay."

He gushed with pleasure.

"Awww, don't worry about me, Bev. I'm lucky; I've got you around to make me look good."

Oh, Clay, you have no idea how lucky you really are.

I went off to find Anthony.

32

ANTHONY

IF I ASKED, I wondered if I could get Alicia to be my stylist for the rest of my life.

I mean, I looked good. I looked *really* good.

The flannel shirt hung widely enough that I looked a little broader. She'd done something to my hair that made my head look leaner. More dangerous.

I spread my stance, angled my face, and struck a pose. I couldn't believe it. I was handsome. How had nobody noticed this before?

Beverly opened the door to my dressing room.

God, I must look like such an idiot. I quickly turned away from the mirror, reverted back to my normal posture, and was reminded of how my stealth handsomeness had remained unnoticed for so long.

"Beverly. Hey."

She didn't answer me right away. She closed the door behind her and lingered in the doorway with her hands crossed demurely behind her back. Her eyes started low and then worked their way up my body until they were locked onto mine.

"Hey," she said.

She'd said hello to me before. Since rehearsals had started, she'd greeted me and bid me farewell with alarming regularity.

The way she was talking to me now was different. It wasn't just "Hey." It was "*Hey.*"

I tried not to read anything into it, I was still worried about jumping the gun and ruining whatever chance I had with her, but it wasn't easy. Especially after dress rehearsals started and she was looking at me every day like she was supposed to be my girlfriend....

Get real, I reminded myself. *I mean that literally. Don't let the costumes fool you, you're still in the real world.*

Then she started walking towards me and suddenly it wasn't the real world at all.

Because it wasn't just her voice that was different now, it was everything. Her walk was different, her eyes were different.

And it was all so unbelievably, incredibly hot.

The Beverly I knew was beautiful and confident and enchanting but this...*thing* coming towards me was more breathtaking and irresistible than anything I'd ever seen anywhere. Porn, movies, paintings, they all seemed dull and washed out compared to what was right here in front of me, so close that I could reach out and touch it if I dared.

And she wanted me. I could feel it coming off of every controlled, deliberate flex of leg and swing of hip. It hit me in waves of mad desire like nothing I'd ever known before. It was even clearer in her bright blue eyes. It was like the way she looked onstage when she was pretending to be my girlfriend only now it was so much stronger. She was looking at me like she wanted me, right then and there, more than anything she'd ever wanted in her entire life.

And I wanted to run.

I wanted her so badly. I'd never want anything as much as I wanted her at that moment, but I still wanted to run away and never look at her ever again.

There was too much coming off of her. Too much heat. Too much power.

It was terrifying, that's the only word I can think of for the sheer hunger I saw coming out of those eyes and that slow, deliberate walk.

I stayed because I'd waited too long for her to look at me like that to run now. I didn't even care if it killed me.

"Showtime yet?" I couldn't care less about the show but I needed to say something because I couldn't take the raw electricity that was building up in the silence of that hip swinging, slinking strut.

33

BEVERLY

"Not yet," I answered without slowing my executioner's stride.

I'd already decided I was going to make it quick before I made it ugly. Anthony didn't need to suffer for me to get my point across.

It just had to look like he had.

My hands were still behind my back. I slid the four-inch nail out from the waistband of my hotpants and shuffled it into position.

"Don't worry, everything's fine, Anthony."

I was going to slam the nail quickly into his ear. He wouldn't even know what had happened to him. There'd be a loud pop, a blood blossom in his right eye, and then he would drop and I would be able to really get started.

"I just need to..."

I leaned in close. I wanted to be sure that I wouldn't miss.

And then he kissed me.

Not a little cheek peck like Clay did. He threw his whole body into it. Kissed me with everything he had.

I dropped the nail. Neither of us heard it over the thunder of his lips pressing against mine.

And it was not a lone sensation of pressure either. His lips were moving against mine. His hands were cupping my face. I could taste the faint remnants of a slice of pizza on his tongue.

And then, he abruptly pulled back. He couldn't have looked more pained if I had stabbed him.

"You're not...," I started without being able to finish. I was too stunned. I couldn't order my thoughts well enough to express them.

Anthony had a different problem.

"Oh, God. I'm so sorry. I thought that- I mean, you were all- and I- then I- I'm such an idiot. Please, don't think that I'm-"

This time, I kissed him.

I didn't see why I shouldn't. If he wasn't gay, then there really wasn't any reason to kill him. And since I was already here, there was something fulfilling in his kisses that was missing from the slobbering, cannibalistic onslaught of the guys I usually hooked up with. I might as well enjoy it.

I grabbed his collar with both hands. The more I kissed him, the more I wanted to keep kissing him. His lips were like a song that got stuck in your head. The kind of stuck where you'd burn out the playback button on your iTunes listening to it a hundred times in a row.

That was how I felt at that moment. It only got more intoxicating when Anthony got over his shock and put his hands on me again. Instead of my face, this time he got one hand around the small of my back, the other against my shoulder, and pulled me tight against him. I went with it and yanked him tighter against me. His kisses, they were frantic but lingering, firm but not forceful. My God, where did he learn to-

Loud thundering at the door.

"ANTHONY! SHOWTIME!"

Alicia. That cliterfering bitch.

The pounding brought Anthony back to reality. I looked into his wide eyes and smiled.

"I guess we're going to have something to talk about after the show."

Before he could start stuttering, I leaned in and hit 'repeat' again.

34

THE PLAY OPENED ON SCHEDULE. The whole cast came out for the opening song and everybody was still alive and in one piece.

And we were good. Better than I think anyone expected us to be. Sometimes people work better when something's for real than they do when it's just practice. That's what happened with our performance. Background dancers who could never seem to sync up leapt across the rooftop stage in perfect unison. High notes that supporting players could never quite reach were hit with ease.

And Anthony and I? The doomed love story upon which everything else revolved?

We were perfection.

After what happened in his dressing room, we couldn't not be.

Not that I actually loved him, but I couldn't be this close to him without remembering how he'd made my heart pound and my body thirst. My desire for him infused my every gesture, look, and word for the entire audience to see.

It was the same for Anthony. When he held me on stage, the audience could feel how badly he wanted to throw me down and ravage me right there.

He didn't miss a step after I left the stage either. I watched him and Clay go through their first duet from the stage right eaves.

Consummate professional, that boy was.

Alicia came up beside me. Emotions were running high all around, her ecstasy at how well the play was going was easily the equal of anything Anthony and I felt for each other. She was smiling as she watched them perform.

"They actually make a cute couple," she said, looking at them not unkindly. "Maybe I should have cast them as Corey and Thromson instead."

I was smiling too. I couldn't seem to stop. "I think Anthony might have had some problems with that." I said. Stupid, now she was going to ask-

"What do you mean?"

I shouldn't have said anything. I didn't know why I even wanted to. I'd never talked about guys with her and Lyndsay before. Not dead ones and certainly not live ones.

"I mean he's not gay." And then I couldn't help it. "And he's not a bad kisser either."

Her jaw dropped.

"No way. You didn't."

I giggled.

"In his dressing room before you knocked."

She was flabbergasted. "You've got to be kidding me. We could have fed him to your last boyfriend!"

"I know. He's skinny. And he's... an intellectual."

"Is that what we're calling it now?"

I ignored her. "But he's also really sweet. And funny. I don't know, maybe my tastes are maturing."

"Maybe," Alicia said. "Or maybe there's some weird airborne disease going around."

She directed my attention to where Lyndsay was still working it and Curtis was clearly very happy to let himself be worked.

"But at least that I can sort of get after the whole Mr. Hughes mess," Alicia went on. "You know Heather? She broke up with that one jerk and then went lesbo? Same principle."

"And what about me?"

I was turning back to look at her.

As I did, I noticed a folding utility knife on the ledge beside her head.

Alicia had already turned her attention back to the stage, apparently bored of our love lives. "If this is part of the Columbia 'clean slate' thing you were talking about, then your priorities are even more fucked than I thought."

"Still not on board?" My hand was creeping towards the knife as we talked.

Alicia didn't notice. "Not even a little bit. But I know he's going to Caltech so at least this batshit comes with an expiration date."

I stopped with my hand on the handle of the blade.

"Oh."

I hadn't even thought of that.

Alicia whirled on me without warning.

Just as quickly, I made the knife disappear into my cleavage. I tucked it in sideways, deep under the breast where the bulge wouldn't show.

"You're not thinking of going long distance with him?" she asked accusingly. "Are you?"

I shook my head firmly.

"No. Clean slate, remember?"

The weight of the knife close to my heart was all the reminder I needed.

Satisfied, Alicia went back to the show.

"Good. Just make sure you erase him too when you do. Now hurry up, your cue's coming soon."

She was right, Clay and Anthony's song was coming to its conclusion. I went behind the faux door. It was a wooden vestibule that led into the apartment set. Nobody was there but me.

There, alone in the dark, I waited for my solo.

After the song, Clay came through the door. That was the end of the scene. I was supposed to wait a beat, then I'd enter and sing a number of my own.

Clay took the moment of our two ships passing in the night to smile broadly. "Heyyy, Bever-"

I clamped a hand over his mouth and slashed the knife across his throat.

The wound was a second mouth, blood sprayed everywhere. Especially on me.

I took my hand off his mouth. The air would escape from the gaping wound in Clay's throat before it would leave his mouth as a scream. I grabbed him by the neck for balance, stuck my thumb in his slashed throat so I wouldn't lose my grip, and attacked him in a flurry of slashes.

I wasn't enjoying this as much as I wanted to, but I didn't have the time. If I was lucky, I had a minute before someone came to see why I'd missed my cue. There was no room for pleasure because there was no room for errors. Every cut had to be more right than I could make it if I was just having fun.

In the end, what I did was serviceable for a rush job. It wasn't quite up to my usual standards, but I thought the audience would eat it up.

All it needed was the final touch.

35

ANTHONY

A MINUTE WENT by in dead silence. I had no idea what I was supposed to be doing. Maybe a tap routine?

And then, from off stage, there was the heavy thud of a fist against wood. Somebody knocking on the door wasn't in the script but I got the point.

"Hang on, coming!"

There was another loud, impatient knock from the other side of the door.

36

BEVERLY

I SLAMMED my head against the side of the set again. My skin had split from the first impact, but the slight burn and thin trickle of blood I felt running down my cheek didn't feel like enough.

The pain was greater now, the wetness on the side of my face was thicker.

I heard Anthony. "Hang on, coming!"

I smashed my head into the wood beam one more time for good measure. Alicia always said that less is not more when it came to the theatre.

37

ANTHONY

I RUSHED to answer the door, relieved that things were back on track.

The dead body actually didn't swing that much when I opened the door. The toes of his shoes barely grazed my shins.

I would have nightmares about those brown moccasins for the rest of the year. In the worst ones, I was wearing them and they wouldn't come off no matter how hard I pulled at them.

But I saw Clay. I saw that his eyes, ears, and nose were all slashed to red ruins. I saw the long, bloody gashes cut from wrist to elbow on both arms. At first, I didn't realize what he was hanging from, but then it hit me. *It's his scarf.* His white scarf that wasn't white anymore. One end was still wrapped around his neck. The other was tied to the support beam behind the doorway.

I could hear the crowd too. Screams and horror and cries for 911.

Thirty seconds. Not even enough time to watch a whole YouTube video but more than enough time to realize how absolutely terrifying it was to be dead.

Time enough to read too.

FAG

SOMEONE HAD CARVED IT INTO HIS CHEST. THREE LETTERS. ELEVEN slash marks. The singular horror of motive.

It took thirty-one seconds to see Beverly. I was being ushered away by someone then. It might have been Mr. Hodder; he was my honors bio teacher who never had much of a problem with blood. I couldn't tell for sure because as soon as I saw Beverly on the ground I was fighting like a lunatic to get back to her.

"Beverly! BEVERLY!"

She was bleeding. I could see that but I couldn't see if she was alive or dead.

"Let me go! Beverly, can you hear me?!"

I had to help her. I'd kissed her. Another teacher was trying to pull me away by then and I was kicking and scratching at both of them. I'd kissed her. Didn't they understand that?

I elbowed someone in the nose. Was it blood that wet my face or was it my own tears?

Beverly. Oh, Beverly.

The school nurse had finally made her way through the crowd. She was crouched beside Beverly with two fingers pressed to her throat. I watched her stand and shout out into the crowd.

"She's alive! Someone call an ambulance!"

Alive.

I slumped in the arms of the teachers and allowed them to carry me away. I don't think I ever passed out but I do think I slipped into shock. All I can say is I grayed out for the next two hours and when I was coherent again, the thought was stronger. As if I'd been nursing it that entire time.

Alive.

Thank you, Jesus. Alive.

BEVERLY

I CAME TO AND THERE WAS SOMEONE SOBBING RIGHT IN MY EAR.

Not that I'd ever been unconscious. I'd been awake with my eyes closed for all of the screaming and sirens and madness of the murder scene, but I'd dozed off on the ambulance ride to the hospital.

I kept my eyes closed. In the darkness, I tried to see if I could pinpoint who it was weeping over my grievous injuries. Lyndsay was the front runner, but it might have been Alicia. Or maybe even Anthony. Though, really, we'd just kissed once. Give me some space.

I heard the sound of a chair scraping the floor. Someone was moving closer to console the mourner.

"I know," my dad said.

My dad? That would make the weeper...

No. No way.

"She's just so QUIET," my mom wailed.

My God. It was her. My mom was *crying*.

She was still talking. I had to strain to hear her through the sobs. "And the nurses tucked her in. I keep thinking that she looks like she used to when she was a little girl. Remember? We always had to tuck her in before she'd go to sleep."

He chuckled softly. "I remember."

"And she always wanted you to tell her a story." The *"never me,"* went unsaid but we all heard it.

"I just did the voices better," my dad said.

A memory I never even knew I had flashed against the screen of my eyelids. Me in pink princess pajamas with clean sheets pulled up to my chin, spellbound as my dad replicated an amazing range of voices. High and low, fast and slow, as he led me through the adventures of *The Stinky Cheeseman and other Fairly Stupid Tales.*

"Run, run, run as fast as you can. You can't catch me-" He tweaked my nose and blew a raspberry in my face. *"I'm the stinky cheeseman!"* I giggled and playfully pushed him away. He responded by wrapping

me in a hug, the book squished between us, and kissing the top of my head. I heard him sigh adoringly against my hair.

It's amazing that something could be so vivid and at the same time feel like it happened to an entirely different person.

My mom laughed through her tears. She sniffled.

Silence between them.

Then, a muffled sound I couldn't quite pick out.

A small, breathy gasp.

The same sound again. This time, I was able to place it.

Kissing.

I snapped my eyes open, forgetting I was supposed to feign a gradual return to consciousness from a savage beating instead of springing awake after a refreshing nap. I couldn't help it.

Luckily, now they were the ones with their eyes closed, lost in each other's feeling and taste. I hadn't seen them kiss like that in years. I don't know how long they would have gone on like that. Maybe all night; maybe they would have gone further (which, ew) but I wasn't going to find out. Now that I'd seen it for myself I was remembering where I was and what I was supposed to do.

I closed my eyes again, found my center like Alicia taught us during rehearsals, and let out a disoriented groan.

"Beverly?"

My eyes fluttered open. My parents weren't kissing anymore, they were crowded around my bedside, full of fear, concern, and then relief as I gradually returned to the land of the living.

"Mom? Dad?"

"We're here, baby," my mom said. One hand held mine. The other snaked out and took my father's.

"Both of us."

I acted confused and felt the stitched wound on my forehead, as if I didn't know how it had gotten there. "What's going on? Did something happen to-"

I shuddered as if the memory had just hit me. My eyes watered. "No. No, Oh my- I-" I covered my mouth and tried to curl up in bed like I felt dirty and horrified with remembrance.

"They killed him."

My dad stroked my arm and I flinched away as if I'd been cut.

"Beverly-"

I squeaked like it was all I could do not to scream.

"There were two of them. They came up behind us. They were laughing, I thought they were just assholes playing a prank but..."

I couldn't finish. I was too panicked. Too terrified by just the memory. My dad pulled me into a hug and stroked my hair. In that moment, I was really reliving it as if I hadn't been the one doing the killing.

"Shhhh. You're safe, Beverly. No one's here but us. I promise."

I wiped my eyes, trying to take control of myself.

"I saw their faces. I didn't recognize them but I can tell you what they look like."

"Don't worry about that right now," he shushed. "You just woke up. We need to make sure you're alright."

"But don't you always say that the first few hours after a crime are the most critical part of an investigation."

"Yes, but-"

"Then stop treating me like your daughter and start treating me like a witness." My dad looked at me carefully. I let my fear and vulnerability show through in my eyes and the quiver of my lip and let my posture and my raised chin convey my strength.

"Alright."

He changed too. He sat back in his seat and grabbed a pad off my nightstand as if he'd never laid eyes on me before.

"You said there were two of them?"

I nodded. "They were older than us. College maybe."

"What did they look like?"

"They were both tall. One of them was latino, the other was white. They both had shaved heads. I didn't know anything was wrong; they looked so normal."

"They always do. Did you notice anything else?"

I thought about it for a moment. The trick to looking confused was to think about something you actually didn't know so I tried to divide twelve by eleven hundred in my head.

Finally, I shook my head.

"I don't know. It happened so fast. They grabbed Clay and when I tried to stop them one of them grabbed me and... and..."

My dad had heard enough. He got out of the chair and he was my dad again.

"That's ok," he told me. "You did great. Tomorrow, well get a sketch artist in here. Tonight, I want you to get some rest, ok? There's going to be an officer outside all night, nobody's going to hurt you."

My mom squeezed my hand. "The doctor left a sleeping pill in case you woke up. Do you want it?"

I nodded meekly. I must have looked drained. My mom handed me the pill and a glass of water. I took it. "We're going to stay right here, honey." I nodded and leaned back like the pill was already taking effect. My eyes fluttered.

"Good night, mommy."

She held back tears.

"Good night, baby."

And.... scene.

Darkness again. I heard them talking.

My dad first. "I...." he sounded guilty.

"You have to go be a cop," my mom didn't sound critical.

"I just need to call in these descriptions and see if anything turned up at the school," he said as if she had. "Then I'll-"

"Find the animals who did this. We'll be waiting."

I heard another kiss.

"Both of us."

Footsteps and a door opening and closing. I wasn't asleep yet, but I could feel it tugging at me. That pill was something else.

But I earned it. After everything with Anthony blew up in my face (literally. In my face.) I had thought about scrapping the whole plan. Alicia would just have to make do with a DJ.

Instead, I slashed both of Clay's wrists while he waved his arms all over the place. I cut off his nose and his ears and his eyes while he struggled and spasmed. And then I took the knife to his chest. Cutting words into a person is like writing on an old typewriter or filling out a college application in ink. Make a typo and you had to throw the whole thing out.

I came up with all of that carnage when I thought I'd have five whole minutes and a dressing room all to myself.

And onstage I didn't have the option of just slipping away either. Faking a head injury was just as risky as the killing. If it didn't look good enough my story would be examined much more closely. If it looked too good... well, a double murder would have made us a shoo-in for the Kincaids show.

Total silence, complicated knife work, no way to escape. To take on all of that in a glorified closet with a window of less than a minute was....

Was the reason why I loved to do what I did.

Because I had a gift.

I smiled in my "sleep." I felt my mother kiss my brow.

Who cares if the play didn't go more than ten minutes? I'd put on the best show of my life.

38

ANTHONY

WHEN THE MEMORIAL WAS READY, they asked Beverly if she would feel comfortable saying a few words. Everyone knew how close she and Clay were. It was a rare good decision by the administration that was best known for "Hug a Friend Fridays."

One day after rehearsal, Beverly had told me about how she thought acting was like a mirror ball. This wasn't exactly acting, but I was seeing another side of her nonetheless: Beverly the leader. There was so much fear and confusion running through the school after Clay was murdered. Our campus was in one of the sunniest places in the world, but with the auditorium doors still tied shut with police tape, it felt like there were shadows everywhere.

Sure, the police said that the killers were outsiders, burnouts without the grades for college or the temperament for work, but we didn't *know* that. People were quieter in the hallways. Everyone looked at each other a little more guardedly. The idea that, just maybe, there was a killer sitting next to you in third period was on everybody's mind but nobody's lips.

It was fear. Fear and hurt. Clay had been killed but we'd all been cut and there wasn't a guidance counselor or therapist in the whole state that could convince us that we could walk around without bracing ourselves for another cut.

But there was Beverly.

This memorial for Clay was the first time the whole student body had been together since the night of the play. It was out in the courtyard and, as the rest of us arrived, Beverly was already there. She stood on a makeshift podium in front of a wall cloaked in a white sheet. There was a large bandage wrapped around her head. Seeing it was a reminder that we could moan about our damaged feelings all we wanted, but Beverly was the only one of us who'd been lucky to get away with her life. And seeing her up there, the wound on her head so prominent but so plainly insignificant to her, it reminded all of us that it was possible to get hurt and keep on going.

And that was before she even began to speak.

"...I know how strong the temptation is to hate the people behind this heinous act," she was saying. "But hatred is the reason that we're here today. Here, in mourning, and not with our friend Clay by our side."

"Clay Harris did not know how to hate. What he understood was goodwill. Love. Friendship. If we came here today to honor Clay, than hatred is the last thing any of us should feel in our hearts."

Her statement was greeted by nods and applause. Not just from the social justice, vegan crusaders. From the kids who usually didn't even show up to these things.

"In that spirit, Clay's spirit, a ballot was distributed earlier this week proposing that we donate this year's prom fund to establish an anti-hate foundation named in Clayton Alexander Harris' name. I'm proud to say that this motion passed by a landslide."

Even more applause. And it was honest applause. I'm sure every kid who voted aye on that ballot knew that, once word got out, the MVC was going to throw us a prom three times more lavish than anything even the cream of Beverly Hills could raise with car washes and school plays.

But that's not why any of us made the choice we did. What

happened to Clay was genuinely disgusting. Everyone was sickened by it, even the people who hadn't even known him.

And I had known Clay. Only for a few months, but that was long enough to know that he was a genuinely good person. He was kind and he knew how to get up after you tried to knock him down and if he'd lived he would have grown up to do something that made the world a better place.

Whoever killed Clay was the opposite of that. They were animals with nothing to contribute to the world but shit and tears. Voting to give away our prom was a small price to pay for a chance to stand up and say that we were better than whoever did this.

"We've learned that there's no predicting tomorrow." Beverly choked back tears. "Every one of us knows the truth of that all too well. Our choice now is to either fear every second of that uncertainty, or to live in defiance of it. That's what we did today. We chose to make our prom into something uncertain. We refused to let our fear of what might or might not happen keep us from doing something to make the world a less hateful place. We did that."

Beverly could have just kept talking, but she knew better. She waited until the applause died down and the somber atmosphere reasserted itself before she continued.

"We did that for Clay. Maybe we can't be certain that he's seeing us right now. We can't even know for sure that he would want a charity named after him. What we can know for sure is that we acted because we loved him. And we miss him. And, now, we can be certain that we'll never forget him."

And that's why Beverly was up there and not me. She felt it too but she knew how to put it into words better than anyone else ever could.

Music came on over the speakers. Something low and acoustic. Beverly reached out and pulled down the curtain. The wall behind her had been repainted. It was a mural now. Clay's face in a wreath of rainbows, a rising sun, and a field of flowers.

A little over the top maybe, but it was the sentiment that mattered.

Beverly knelt beside the podium. There was a box of white roses there. As the music continued, Beverly picked up a rose and took it to the mural. I saw Leo from the school paper snapping away with his camera. The pictures that came out the next day would be phenomenal. Beverly in her simple white dress with a simple white flower, perfectly capturing the beauty and hope that blotted out a red mark that we could have carried with us for the rest of senior year.

The rest of the school fell into line. One by one, we all grabbed a rose from the basket and left it at the base of the mural.

I was one of the last people in line. Story of my life. After I dropped my rose, I saw Beverly by herself at the back of the courtyard. She looked grateful to be unnoticed for a second. I could only imagine how draining it must have been to put yourself on display like that after what had happened to her. I'm sure the last thing she wanted was more attention.

And here I was, still staring at her.

We'd kissed. Before everything had happened with Clay and the night had gone to hell, I was happier than I'd ever been in my life. There would have been an after party at Alicia's house and it would have been the simplest thing in the world to bring Beverly a beer and pick up where we left off.

Now, I had no idea what to do. If I thought having no experience and chasing a girl a thousand miles out of my league was tough, picking up from "Hey, we hooked up and witnessed a brutal murder on the same night," was much worse. You can't even make an emo facebook post about that.

I needed to give her space. That was the right answer. She needed to make her own peace with what happened. She didn't need to see me and be reminded of everything again.

I turned to walk away from her, and that's when I saw Lyndsay and Curtis holding hands.

I already knew about them. The night of the play, while I was traumatized and loaded up on half a dozen Quaaludes, I'd received twelve texts at 3 AM that just said "DUDE." over and over again.

I'd spent three and a half years trying to get Beverly to notice me. I pined and ached and planned and overcame a decade of self-doubt and social disenfranchisement just to get one kiss.

Curtis mentioned that they used to share a kiddie pool, broke into a car, and happened to be there when she needed a hug and parlayed it into a relationship with the second hottest girl in school. He still couldn't walk down the hall without half a dozen strangers reaching out to slap him on the back. Guys were convinced he was Obi-Wan Kenobi. "This *is* the pudgy, ugly guy you're looking for."

I turned back around. To hell with all of that. No way I was being the *Grand Theft Auto 1* to his *Grand Theft Auto 5*.

But that was before I got near her. The closer I got, the less I cared about some stupid macho competition with Curtis. By the time I reached her side, the only thing I cared about was trying to make Beverly feel better. In fact, I'd surprised myself when I realized what I was willing to do for her if I decided that it was the thing that she needed.

"Hey, Beverly."

She smiled thinly. "Hey, Anthony."

I shuffled my feet, wishing I'd thought of something to say before I came over.

"Listen, I'm not going to pretend to know what you're feeling. But if you ever need someone to talk to, or just someone to be there so you're not so... alone." I shrugged. "I'm around."

And if you can't look at me again without remembering what happened, then I'll walk away right now and I won't say a word to you ever again. I'll do that without a single ounce of regret because I love you, Beverly Kilbourne. I love you more than anybody else ever has or ever will.

She shook her head. "I don't need somebody to listen to me cry, Anthony."

"Okay." I nodded. I could have waited long enough for an awkward silence to bloom, but what was the point? That seemed like a firm conversation ender. I turned to go.

She caught my arm.

"What I need," she said, "Is for you to take me somewhere and remind me of the only good thing that happened that night."

"....Seriously?"

Yes, my answer was "Seriously." That was what I had. If you gave me a full week to prepare for that conversation I wouldn't have been able to come up with anything better.

Especially not after she kissed me.

She smiled and brushed a strand of hair away from her eyes, a job that she was going to do for the last time because it was going to be exclusively mine for as long as she'd have me.

"Seriously."

39

BEVERLY

I SAID Anthony's kisses were like a song that got stuck in your head.

And they were, but that wasn't quite right.

They were like a pop song that you couldn't stop listening to even if you only liked hard rock. Or a country song when the rest of your iPod is rap. It's happened to everyone, sometimes you hear a song and it just clicks, no matter what your tastes are.

So, you listen to it. A lot. It gets compulsive. It gets a little crazy. You're not just listening to the radio, hoping it comes on, you've downloaded the single and you're listening to it four or five times in a row.

And then, one day, you get into the car and that song is the furthest thing from your mind. You put on your metal, or your techno, and you go the rest of your life without thinking about that song ever again.

But, if you were to think about it again, would you be surprised? No. Because even as you're listening to the same song twenty times in a row, you know that newness fades and what's catchy eventually becomes shallow and repetitive. Even when you're dancing to it in the car, you don't mistake it for anything you'll be listening to for the rest of your life because you already know what has meaning to you. You've been listening to it forever. Five years. Ten years. You understand what reaches out to you and makes you understand the world and your place in it. You know what to play that has a message you'd post online or carve on your tombstone.

I knew what my calling was and I knew that, as good of a kisser as Anthony was, his body didn't feel as perfect in my hands as a knife handle did.

But so what? I was seventeen; nobody I knew was in a relationship that was going to make it past next spring semester. I had three months to kill in Los Angeles (no pun intended). If I was going to be here, and he was going to be here, and I liked being with him, then there was no reason not to let him get stuck in my head for awhile. Not so long as I didn't pull a Lyndsay and set the rest of my universe around a good fuck.

Also.....

Also, with my parents apparently not splitting up I was missing another really good reason to not want to come back to LA.

"Witnessing" Clay's murder was a good start. But if I were to lose someone else people thought I was close with? A boyfriend for example? I couldn't be an auxiliary victim again, that would be too much coincidence for anyone to ignore, but an accident could work. Or maybe a senseless killing when I could arrange for a passable alibi.

Either way, if something gruesome were to happen where I could attend a closed casket service and wear a funeral veil so thick that nobody could see my smile behind it?

If that happened, why, who could expect the poor thing to ever want to come back West? Of course she'd rather stay in New York. Besides, she does seem happy whenever we talk to her.

I wondered if Anthony had a habit of keeping electronics near the shower. Or if he liked to go hiking through mountain passes with steep drops?

I considered the skinny legs in the driver's seat next to me. Probably not.

They were cute little legs though.

But I was getting ahead of myself. As we pulled into the Baja Burger parking lot, I gave his hand a squeeze and watched him throw himself out of the car in his haste to open my door for me. I told myself to have a good time and stop worrying so much.

I had all summer to kill him.

INTERLUDE FIVE:

SCHOOL'S OUT

If Clive Spencer were sober, he would feel like the asshole of the universe right now.

That was not an exaggeration. A sober Clive would look at himself in this exact moment and feel like the terminus point where the collective shit of the universe funneled out.

This isn't really him. He doesn't walk around with an extra-large slice of chest hair hanging out of his shirt. He has no idea what to do with styling putty. He went to a club once before and only stayed as long as he did because if he paid twelve dollars for a beer then goddamnit he was going to finish it.

But, Clive Spencer is not that same person anymore. That person was with Ashley. That person thought he was on the right track and having her in his life was what he got for making as many correct calls as he did.

None of that is true anymore. Ashley has broken up with him and, if doesn't want to be with him, then obviously everything about the old Clive was wrong and needs to be eliminated with extreme prejudice.

So, Clive went out. He bought a shirt that cost more than most of his previous wardrobe combined. He paid a stylist to do his hair.

Not even cut it, just do things to make it shiny and defy gravity. He laid in a tanning bed until his skin was the same shade as an over-cooked pumpkin pie.

Only when he could look in the mirror and completely not recognize himself was he finally satisfied.

Then, he sat in his apartment and got drunk.

When he tried to stand and could barely manage the task, he went to the club.

Now, he's throwing himself across the dance floor at any girl he sees because fuck it. He spent years laughing at the douchebags who go to these places. Now, they're the ones laughing and he's the one with a fiancee who left him for a marketing consultant, quite possibly the douchiest of all professions. Obviously, the douchebags must be doing something right.

And maybe the douchebags are, but Clive is most certainly not doing anything right. Any girl he tries to "grind" with recoils from his touch. He reeks of alcohol. His hands go too quickly to the breasts or crotch, even for this crowd. He's one more complaint away from being forcibly taught some manners when a girl finally responds to his affections.

Impossibly, it's the most beautiful girl in the entire club. Her face is half covered by a down-tilted fedora but, even made stupid by alcohol and regret, Clive can see enough of her to realize just how amazing it is for this girl to even touch him. And yet she is. When his hands slide to fondle her breasts, she doesn't just approve, she presses his hands even tighter to her chest and grinds her hips against his until his groin overcomes a truly heroic amount of whiskey to mount a full erection.

And then she turns and kisses him.

Clive kisses back. His technique is atrocious. He doesn't so much kiss her as bathe her with his tongue like a newborn kitten. He doesn't care. Gorgeous as she is, this isn't about this girl. It's about Ashley and how much she hurt him when she left. He actually wishes she was here because, truthfully, Ashley's front teeth were crooked and her ass was narrow. This girl he's kissing is a goddess and Clive wants Ashley to see just how high he's climbed and how much of an idiot she was to leave him.

He's so ecstatic that it actually takes him almost a minute to realize he's also feeling blinding pain.

His tongue to be exact. She's biting him. Clive's not into that. He tries to pull away.

Beverly grabs his head with fingers like talons and holds him where he is.

She keeps kissing him. Her teeth sink deeper into his tongue. Blood's smearing around his mouth along with the red of her lipstick. Clive tries to break loose but he's drunk and while Beverly isn't overly muscled, she has the feral strength of any hunter when it's making a kill.

When she has a firm grip on his tongue, Beverly yanks it from his head.

Clive recoils. He's no longer thinking about Ashley. She's been eclipsed by the fire burning in his head and the sensation of blood filling his mouth. There's no taste because his tongue is gone but he feels the blood pooling like water flowing from a burst pipe.

My tongue. My tongue, oh my God my fucking tongue!

Then, survival takes over. He stumbles away from her.

Beverly stalks after him. But first, she spits the torn remnants of Clive's tongue onto the dance floor.

She's not a cannibal.

In the flashing lights, writhing bodies, and pounding bass of the club, nobody has heard any screams or noticed anything out of the ordinary. Clive's frantic steps are mistaken for someone rushing to the bathroom before they throw up.

Blindly, he reaches out for help. The first girl he touches grabs his arms and wraps them around her waist. She grinds against him.

Of course. Now he finds a girl who welcomes his advances.

Blood is still pouring from the savage wound where his tongue was and the girl is shorter than him. Blood drips on her head. The girl mistakes it for saliva and pushes him away in disgust.

Clive tumbles to the floor, off balance and woozy with blood loss. He starts to crawl. As he does, he reaches for his cellphone. He's trying to call Ashley. Deprived of thought by panic and bleeding, it is Ashley he reaches out to as he always had when he was hurt or in trouble.

Too much of his blood has splattered over the phone. He can't access his contact list through the tacky film covering the touch screen.

He moans pathetically, but it can't be heard over the music. He hammers at the number icons, hoping fervently that it's going through. He holds the phone to his ear, desperately praying he'll hear something.

Ringing. Faint with all the sound behind him, but it's there. And then it's not just ringing. It's Ashley's voice.

"I told you to stop calling me, Clive."

He tries to tell her he needs help, needs her to save him as she always has, and realizes too late the futility of what he's done.

He doesn't have a tongue.

He groans into the phone anyway. They were together five years. Even if she doesn't love him anymore, she'll know something's wrong. And she'll get help. She'll find him. She'll save him.

"Listen, Clive."

And then a stiletto heel specially sharpened for just such a purpose stabs through the base of his skull and severs it from his spinal column.

Clive gasps and twitches. Beverly jerks her leg to the side, completely shattering his spine but also breaking off the heel of her shoe.

Fuck.

Nobody's noticed Clive yet, but they will soon. Beverly tugs the hat down further over her eyes and takes off her shoes. She walks out of the club with her heels dangling from one finger. When she gets to a dumpster, she'll toss them. She has flip flops in her car. Until then, she'll look like just another girl going barefoot after a night of dancing too hard.

Inside of the club, unaware of the dead connection, Ashley's still on the line.

"I know you're hurting, but think about it. Could I make you happy if I was in love with somebody else? Clive, you deserve better than that!"

Of course, no answer. Ashley sighs. "I let you go so someone else could find you. I promise you, Clive, even if I'm not the person you want to hear it from, there's someone out there who can do for you what no one else ever could. You just need to wait a little longer for her to find you."

40

Things finally quieted down after the play.

I went to school. I hung out with Lyndsay and Alicia. I killed a gardener in Malibu with an absolutely ridiculous machine called an electric jaw saw. I went on dates with Anthony. I finally got around to running over a woman with her own Range Rover and it was exactly as satisfying as I'd hoped.

I fell into the routine without complaint. After the roller coaster the rest of the year had been I was happy with the predictability. The only question mark still out was the prom contest. The score needle hadn't moved in any direction in the month since the play. Nobody would actually come out and say it but everyone was surprised that the brutal murder and subsequent charitable donation wasn't good for at least a five-er.

I was more annoyed than surprised. Compared to the masterpiece I laid down on Clay, Rob Cummings was a strictly by the numbers hack job. If I was going to be recognized for something (you know what I mean), I'd rather it be for something where I showed what I could really do.

But, whatever. If I was interested in getting credit for my work than I was REALLY into the wrong calling. I enjoyed killing both of them; that was what mattered. If I felt like I deserved a reward, I didn't need anyone to give me that either.

We'll agree to that, the cellar voices chimed in. *Take a night to yourself, Bev. You earned it. Paint the town red.*

Well, if I insisted.

I threw everything I needed into my bag and then checked myself out in the mirror. My hair was pulled back into a bun, I was wearing a nice-looking denim shorts and tank top combo, I had my gloves in my bag.

And my phone beeped as a text came in. But, it beeped on my desk and not in my bag, which is exactly where I wanted it. Fun fact: cell phones record where you're going even when you're not actually using them. Leaving my phone on my desk was the digital equivalent of stuffing pillows under the blanket when you snuck out.

I spun the phone a quarter clockwise and picked it up so I could see who it was. Lyndsay.

"What's up tonight?"

I set the phone down without answering it. I'd tell her later that my battery was dead.

Then the call came. Alicia. I didn't even need to answer it because I knew it would just be the answer to Lyndsay's question: "Sick party tonight! Come now! You're a bitch if you don't!"

Except it wasn't Alicia. It was Anthony. I hesitated. I was just going to let it go to voicemail but I decided to pick it up on the last ring. The least I could do was tell him I was busy.

"Hey, Beverly. What's cookin' good lookin'?"

I giggled. He was so cheesy.

"Not much," I grabbed my purse. "Just hanging around here."

"Did Lyndsay text you yet?"

"No," I lied. "Why?"

"I was talking to her and Curtis and we were thinking it might be fun to go mini-golfing tonight. Of course, when I say 'fun,' I'm using the post-modern, ironic definition."

He was lucky I was smart, otherwise I'd never laugh at any of his jokes.

He took my laughter for consent. "So, do you want me to pick you up? New stereo in the El Camino. The bass notes sound like bass now."

"....I don't know, Anthony. I'm not feeling so good."

I've also already seen you twice this week. I've also got the weight of my purse on my shoulder and I know why it's so heavy and that weight is not something you can compete with so don't even try to make me feel bad.

"Oh. That's cool."

No, it wasn't. I heard the bashful silence of the person I'd shared a locker wall with for three years come roaring back in every word he said.

Worse, I heard him trying to act like he didn't realize it.

"Well," He said, "You know, it's your call. But they're not going 'til eight so if you change your mind, let me know and we'll catch up with them."

Change your mind. Not "feel better." Change your mind.

"I will," I said. "I'll see you soon, Anthony."

"I know," he said, though I very much doubted that he really believed it. "Bye, Bev."

He hung up. I put the phone down and just stood there, listening to the silent ticking of my own brain.

I started walking to the door.

I stopped without thinking.

I went back to the phone. Dialed. Waited.

"What's up?" He was trying to be cool but the phone only rang once before he picked up.

"That offer to change my mind still good?" I asked.

"Definitely!"

I could hear the smile in his voice. I hoped he could hear mine. "Call when you're getting close. Bye, Anthony."

We hung up. I went back to the dresser with my bag. I set it down and took out the claw hammer I'd been planning to use that night. I opened the drawer to put it away.

Stick it underneath my iPad. Use it later. Later tonight even.

I couldn't put the hammer down.

It was titanium. Fifty dollars more expensive than the others for sale but when I swung it at the store it was so light and fast and the clerk assured me it packed the same punch as steel. I wanted to see what it could do to a person's face. I wanted to hit someone just right in the temple and see if it could make the entire side of their face shatter. And that was just the head. There were also broken ribs to think about. Spines. Fingers. Kneecaps. There was internal damage: organs pulverized to soup. Collapsed tracheas.

Was I really going to trade all of that for a mini-golf club?

I shoved the hammer into the drawer. Over my iPad, not under it. I heard the screen crack.

I didn't care. I slammed the drawer shut. Everything on my dresser wobbled. An open bottle of nail polish fell and spilled before I could catch it.

"SHIT!"

The polish ran down my desk and onto the floor. It drip, drip, dripped into a steadily growing pool that I was powerless to clean up.

It was red.

I left it where it was. I went down to the living room and sat with my parents until Anthony came to get me.

My mom asked me to get her a bottle of water from the kitchen and I refused.

I didn't want to go near that many knives.

41

"DON'T MESS UP."

Lyndsay ignored him. She kept her focus on the small green ball in front of her feet.

"Don't mess up."

Admirably, she was still lining up her shot.

"Donn'tttt messss upppp."

The sing-song was too much. Lyndsay looked up. She tried to look stern but the half-grin ruined the whole effect.

Standing behind her, Curtis looked back innocently. "What? I'm saying DON'T mess up."

I never had that much respect for Lyndsay. Never disliked her, obviously thought she was perfectly hot, but she was still one of those people who didn't know that the *Titanic* was a real boat before it was a movie.

Still, seeing her with only minimal makeup, smiling at Curtis because she could see past his looks to the person who wanted to make her laugh, if I wasn't already so madly in love with Beverly...

Lyndsay's turn was last. Beverly and I were on a bench flanked by colored lanterns while we waited to go to the next hole. Beverly was sitting in my lap, idly running her fingers up and down the back of my neck, and I didn't care if we never moved. I was a little worried about Beverly though. When I picked her up she'd been shaking and she hadn't talked too much. Even now, she looked a little pale.

I remembered what she said about not feeling well. I thought she'd just been trying to blow me off but I hoped she wasn't really sick and forcing herself to go out because I'd made her feel bad.

Lyndsay finally took her shot. She'd lined it up right but she'd obviously hit it too hard. Even from here I could see she was going to overshoot the hole.

"No, no, no!"

That was Curtis. He sprinted forward, pumping his legs with determination and cardio that I honestly didn't think he had. He raced the ball to the hole and won.

"YOU. SHALL. NOT. PASS."

He planted his putter handle first into the hole like Gandalf stabbing his staff into the bridge in the Mines of Moira. The small, green, not at all terrifying, Balrog that was the golf ball hit the shaft of Curtis' putter and plunged into the 3-inch abyss with a dull "plunk."

Lyndsay whooped jubilantly and hopped over to Curtis. She put her arms around him and planted a big "thank you" kiss on his lips.

Beverly was unmoved. She made a mark on the score pad in her lap.

"I'm marking that down as a three."

"WHAT?!" She and Curtis were both outraged and laughing.

"You don't see Anthony helping me," Beverly said. But she was smiling too.

"That's because he's too uncoordinated," Curtis said dismissively.

"It's because I'm too dignified."

"Dignified? You were the Riddler for Halloween last year." He turned his putter from a staff to a judge's gavel and pointed it accusingly at me. "He was," Curtis said to Beverly directly. "Uncomfortably tight green pants and everything."

"You just quoted *The Lord of the Rings* in front of a girl. In front of your GIRLFRIEND."

I don't have the words to convey how happy we all were that night. If I have the good luck to die in my sleep, I hope that that's the night I'm dreaming of as my heart slows to a stop.

We walked to the next hole. Beverly and Lyndsay were in front, chatting a mile a minute. Curtis and I followed and watched them from behind. We weren't looking at their asses. We were just looking at them.

"When she leaves me next year for some frat guy with a unibrow," Curtis said, "It's gonna destroy me."

"You think she will?"

"Actually, no. I think she really likes me." Curtis was always cheerful so he didn't look or sound any different. But when he laughed you could feel so much more joy trying to explode out of him. "That's the part that's got me convinced I'm going to get decapitated by one of these windmills because I'm pretty sure that's my entire life's supply of good luck right there."

I patted him on the shoulder. "We've done alright, my friend."

"Fuck that. We'd have done alright with a pair of drunken hand-jobs on the tennis court. I don't know what universe we're in where mini-golf beats any kind of contact with my dick, but we're doing way better than alright."

Before I could agree with him, our conversation was interrupted by squeals of glee from Beverly and Lyndsay. But that was alright, all I could really tell him was that he'd summed up what I felt much better than I ever possibly could.

The girls came running back to us.

"That was Alicia," Lyndsay said. "The final point tally came in! We beat JCH!"

"No way!" Curtis yelled.

"Two hundred and twelve to one eighty-five," Beverly said. She wasn't about to burst like Lyndsay was, we were both lukewarm at best about the Kincaids, but she was grinning and she had more of her color back. "And they're going to pay for all of our decorations and everything because we voted to give away our prom fund."

Forget the Kincaids, I was ecstatic we were just getting a prom at all. I was going to go to the prom with Beverly Kilbourne. Bring her a corsage. Pose in her parents' backyard for a dozen awkward photos. Let her witness firsthand what a terrible dancer I was without three months of prep time to rehearse.

Probably ought to actually ask her first.

True. But, when I did, I really believed that she would say yes. The real point was that one of these times, I was going to think that things couldn't get any better and actually be right. Until then, I was going to keep being amazed by how many times I'd been wrong so far.

"Steve Hansen's parents are away so there's a victory party going on there right now," Beverly went on. "You guys want to blow off mini-golf and hit that?"

Curtis pretended to think about it. He held his putter in one hand and his blue golf ball in the other.

"Hmmm. You know, I have spent most of my high school career holding either my stick or blue balls. I think a party might actually be a nice change of pace."

Lyndsay took the club from him. She ran her hand up the shaft suggestively. "Oh, I think it might definitely be a change of pace."

Curtis got very quiet for a moment. Then he started frantically slapping at my pockets.

"Your keys, Anthony. Where are your fucking keys?!"

42

BEVERLY

THE PARTY WAS UNBELIEVABLE.

Not because it was a bro party.

Because it was an everyone party.

Word of our victory in the MVC contest had spread by tweet, tag, and text and it had all converged on this single party. Everyone who had earned a single point for REM throughout the entire year was here.

Bros.

Preps.

Hipsters.

Nerds.

Victims.

It should have been an all-you-can-eat buffet for me. I couldn't stop my eye from noticing them. Every drunk guy who would happily follow my swishing skirt down a dark alley where nobody would be there to see him die. Every girl walking off to get fast food without telling anyone that she was leaving.

Every time I had a thought like that, it seemed like Anthony would be there a second later. Either to ask me if I wanted a drink or just to squeeze my hand or plant a kiss at the corner of my eye.

Surprisingly, he wasn't just sticking to me all night though. Right now, he was talking to Alicia who'd actually stayed friendly, or at least tolerant of him, even after the play had ended. A lot of theatre kids and even plenty of non-theatre kids also knew him well enough to say "hi" to now. And after they did, most of them discovered he was good for more than a single two-letter word.

I sipped my drink and turned my attention back to the beer pong table.

Lyndsay was teaming with Curtis, another wall decoration that was easy to like once you realized he was more than a painting whose eyes followed you wherever you went. They had their opponents down to one cup. Curtis had done most of the work and he teased the two lax players on the other end of the table about the perks of paying attention in geometry.

Lyndsay smiled at him. "After you."

Curtis just bowed formally. "No, no. I insist."

They looked into each other's eyes. They didn't say a word but a moment of perfect sync passed between them. As one, they turned back to the table and lined up their shots.

Inwardly, I winced. Bully for Curtis for trying to make her feel good, but he was in for another four or five rounds of trying to distract their opponents while he waited for Lyndsay to miraculously get one in.

They took a moment to square up. Then, side by side, they shot.

Lyndsay's arm followed his exactly. Her ball's arc mimicked his. Hers landed in the cup a moment after his did.

"I MADE IT!" Lyndsay crowed.

"Yeah, and who was the coach in your corner?" Curtis said. He grabbed her and dipped her. "Gimme some sugar, baby." He leaned in to kiss her.

Then he overbalanced and fell on top of her.

Laughter erupted from the crowd around them, but it wasn't mean. Lyndsay started flopping comically beneath his bulk. "I'm crushed! I'm crushed!" she kept repeating until he cut her off with a dozen kisses that earned more good-natured laughter from the people around them. Even I smiled.

"He stole that line, you know."

Anthony was back beside me, his hand resting comfortably at the small of my back.

I smiled at him. "And I could google everything you've ever said to me and come back empty?"

He winked at me. "I always cite my sources."

I chuckled but I wasn't really paying attention. Over his right shoulder, a couple was fighting. The girl was going to storm off any minute and, if I hurried, I could sweep over her on the dark walk between the party and her car. The houses on this block all had the same, thick, concealing bushes and I had a short coil of barbed wire in my purse. I could wrap it around her throat from behind. She wouldn't be able to scream and no one else would be able to see us. We could have all night.

And then Anthony was tugging at my arm. I looked back to him and his smile wasn't quite there anymore. "Hey, can we talk some-where?" he asked.

Sure. "Talk."

I was looking over his shoulder again. The girl had thrown a drink in her boyfriend's face. She was leaving, but not so fast that I couldn't catch her.

Instead, without even realizing it, I was nodding at Anthony.

"Sure."

But I was still watching the girl disappear into the night.

I led Anthony to the pool house and locked the door behind us. Everyone else would have to wait their turn.

I expected him to immediately start kissing me. Instead, he stayed a respectable distance from me and he kept his hands in his pocket. He looked like he really did just want to talk.

"Is something wrong?" I asked.

I hadn't turned on the lights. The only illumination came from the lanterns by the pool. In the dim light, I saw him shrug.

"No. Not with me. I'm great. It's just... are you ok?"

"I'm fine."

"Yeah. Of course. I'm just saying, you've been in and out."

"I've been a really good hamburger?"

He laughed. "That's what I mean. Sometimes you're like that."

"Like a hamburger."

"Like you're funny," he corrected. "Listening. Here with the rest of us. But then, sometimes I can see you just close the blinds inside your head and walk off to look at something else. I don't know if maybe I did something or if something else is bothering you; but if you want to talk it kind of comes with the boyfriend territory." His eyes got wide. "Not that we've had that talk officially or that's how I think of myself or that's how I expect you to think of me."

I loved it when he babbled. Less so when I had things I didn't want him to pry at. I put a finger to his lips so he'd stop talking. I smiled at him.

"It's nothing."

"But there is an 'it'?"

Apparently there had to be or else he was never going to let this go. Like all good actresses, I turned to some real life experience for inspirstion.

"Principal Vernon called me into his office today," I said. "He asked me to give the Valedictorian speech."

"Really? Good deal."

I didn't answer. I cast my eyes to the floor and bit my lower lip. I waited for him to draw it out a little more and draw himself in deeper.

"...Bad deal?"

"It should be your speech," I protested. "You've got the highest GPA in the grade. And you're going to Caltech." As if those were the reasons I didn't want to give the speech about an experience that meant nothing to me to an audience full of people I didn't care about.

"So?"

...So, you accept when I ask you to do the speech. You also assume that's what I was really upset about and then we stop talking about it and go back to the party or we stay here and make out. Either way, just please stop picking at things you could never understand.

Anthony didn't try to leave. He didn't try to kiss me either. He squeezed my hands instead.

"Your average is almost as high as mine," he said. "And you're going to Columbia. And you were head cheerleader and you were one of the leads in the-"

He hesitated, not wanting to bring up the play for fear it would upset me.

He took me into his arms. I sunk into them deeper than I wanted to.

"The point is that the Valedictorian is supposed to represent the whole class. That's you. You're the spirit of this place. I was just a ghost roaming the halls."

I shook my head. Not caring about distracting him, only caring that he still thought like that.

"Anthony-"

"I'm not feeling sorry for myself," he said. "I've... I've got you. And that means more to me than a speech or anything else ever will."

He didn't back away from me, but his grip loosened, letting me go if I wanted to go.

"I know it's stupid. I know in a few months we're going to be on opposite sides of the country. If you want to run away screaming, you can-"

What I wanted to do was kiss him. Kiss him, taste him and feel his body tight against mine until I feel for myself all of whatever it was he felt for me.

So, that's what I did.

I pushed him onto the bed and straddled him, still kissing him wildly. He was starting to catch up now, kissing me back with that mad need I never felt coming off of anyone else. His hands were on my hips. I grabbed them and guided them to my breasts. When I was sure they weren't going anywhere, I went for his belt.

"Beverly, are you sure you want to do this?"

I kissed him again.

"Shut up, Anthony."

43

BEVERLY AND ANTHONY

I UNDRESSED HER.

I undressed him.

We were still kissing as every layer disappeared. We kissed every newly exposed piece of skin, as if to verify it was really there. Clavicle to hip to leg. To me, every piece was more intoxicating than the last and I realized how lost I really was. No matter what happened after this, there was never going to be another moment of my life where I didn't want to feel her skin against my lips.

I sat up and brought Anthony into a sitting position with me. He came up willingly. He kissed the space between my breasts and then worked his way one kiss at a time to the tip of each one. My nipples ached for him. Everything ached for him. Not just for what he was doing to my skin, but because of the way each kiss reached deeper until it landed on my heart.

I cradled his head. He was so small in my hands. So insubstantial.

I didn't understand how he could feel so strong.

My hands clutched at her back. She was so warm. So alive.

I felt like nothing compared to her.

Still in my lap, she shifted on her knees.

I maneuvered on top of him until I felt his hardness pressing where I needed it. Not inside yet-

-But I was oh so impossibly close. The peak I'd never dreamed of reaching was coming and I was so afraid. I was afraid I'd burst the second I was inside her and a moment I'd want to last forever would be over in seconds.

I wanted to use my fingers first, just to give myself a little longer to prepare, but then the tip of my erection touched something hot and wet. Beverly moaned at the contact and I acted on instinct.

Anthony suddenly surged up. He thrust himself all of the way inside of me.

I screamed.

I screamed.

There were no words for how Anthony felt inside of me because none of them worked. It wasn't size or girth that made him stand out. It was a sense of rightness that filled me. His body was meant for mine, nobody else would ever fit me so perfectly.

"Oh, fuck," I gasped. "Oh, fuck!" I'd never felt anything like this in my whole life. Beverly really was the sun. Exquisite, perfect heat and I knew that I was wrong to have been afraid. I wasn't burning up inside of her. I was burning brighter. I flipped her onto her back and kept sliding in and out of her with wonderful ease. She gasped in time with every stroke and dug her nails into my back.

I drew blood pulling his body tighter against mine. I didn't care. I needed more. I needed him.

"Faster," I begged, pumping my hips along with his. "Faster."

I listened. I was panting but I wasn't tired. I was lost in the sound of our bodies slapping together and the sharp jolt of pleasure that came with each contact. I pushed as deeply into her as I could, every inch was warmer and tighter than the one before it, until our pubic bones were grinding together.

Beverly howled. She grabbed the back of my neck hard and held my head so she could keep us eye to eye. It was like the night in the dressing room all over again, she looked all the way inside of me.

I looked into Anthony's eyes and thought of Frankie and how I'd fallen in love with the sight of life leaving his body.

Now, I watched life rushing into Anthony's. I saw it build inside of him with every roll of my hips against the column of rock inside my body.

And I was matching him pulse for pulse until we were both bursting at the seams.

I couldn't breathe. Or, I could breathe but no amount of air was enough to fuel the fire roaring inside of me.

It didn't matter. I didn't need air.

"Anthony! Anthony!"

I wanted to answer her but I couldn't. The fire was finally boiling me alive. My every nerve ending was scorched raw. The touch of the sheets against my shins was almost sensual enough to make me cum now.

But I still didn't want to. I didn't want to stop feeling this incredible. I didn't want to stop doing things that made Beverly scream my name like it was God's.

So, I withdrew. Not from her, never from her, but from myself. Just enough distance to keep me from losing all control.

I saw him pulling away from me and groped to stop it. I couldn't lose him. I didn't just want the physical sensation, I wanted to stay connected to whatever was racing inside of me.

I rolled over so I was on top. Smashed my lips against his, making sure he tasted them, and then I went to his ear. I got so close that my tongue licked his lobe as I spoke.

"Feel it for me," she whispered.

Straining, I shook my head. Beverly gasped as another wave of pleasure started between her legs and roared through her brain but she recovered and kept rocking faster against me.

"I want you to," she whispered.

I suckled his neck. Right over the pulse point where all of his life rushed.

I exploded.

I felt Anthony erupt inside of me and I lost my name. I lost my memories. Sobbing, laughing, screaming, panting, I lost everything and in its place I knew a joy so intense that it was blinding.

I was still thrusting even as I came. "I love you," I said to her. "I love you. I love you, Beverly. I love, you, I love, I love you."

I collapsed against his chest when I finally couldn't take anymore. Every limb was numb as surely as if my spine had been cut.

"I love you too," I whispered against his sweat soaked skin.

44

BEVERLY

I HELD Anthony close to me, savoring his warm respiration against my chest, enjoying the scentless but clean odor of his cheap shampoo and the perfect weight of his head against my breast.

I could have laid there, still as something in a grave, and never wanted a single thing more.

I held him close to me, loving him so much, and I finally understood the terror others must have felt in their final moment of understanding before I came down with a blade and ripped them away from everything they cared about.

45

I SLIPPED from the tangled sheets while Anthony was sleeping. I quietly dressed myself and slunk away from the bed.

I froze with my hand on the doorknob.

It would be so easy to lie back beside him. Maybe curl myself under his arm instead of the other way around. And if that woke him up, why, we'd just make love again. Not fuck, bang, or have sex. Make Love.

And would it be so perfectly fulfilling the second time around? I had no doubt that it would be.

Steve Harvey was back. *Time for the bonus round, Steve?*

Actually, Beverly. This time we'd like you to be one of our survey takers. Your question is, and remember, we only want your personal top answer.... What if you're not just a killer? What if you actually could be a friend, daughter, and lover and be satisfied with it? What if, all this time, you've just been doing it wrong?

I haven't been.

Really? Would Lyndsay agree? Would Alicia? Your parents? What about the very satisfied boy sleeping behind you?

They're not who I am.

You talk like you don't have a choice.

I don't.

Bullshit, you don't. You got into Columbia without even trying. You're funny, inspiring, gorgeous. My God, you're such an all-around American Beauty it's sickening. So admit it, you have plenty of choices. Come on, Beverly, real number one answer time. You choose to be the despicable, mangy thing that you are… because you like it.

I chose it because I love it. Even if everything else you said is true, all that matters is that I love being what I am.

Maybe if killing is the thing you love the most. But is it really? All this planning you've been doing, putting yourself where nobody else can reach you, separating yourself from everything but blood and screaming. Is that really because all you want to do is binge drink murder? Or are you worried that if you let anything else in you just might like it better?

I bit my lip. On my back, I could still feel the residual warmth from the bed I shared with the man I love.

Outside, I could hear a drunk girl loudly declare she was walking to get Taco Bell by herself.

Beverly? Steve said. I was actually asking you. We need to know what your number one answer is.

….I'll get back to you.

I left the pool house.

46

My return to the party was not unnoticed.

Everyone smiled at me. Everyone greeted me loudly.

They always did, but they were never actually saying hi to me. They were saying hi to breasts and legs and hair and status. They were calling out to whatever it was they wanted from me.

Tonight, I heard their voices but I didn't hear any agendas.

"You're the spirit of this place."

Were they always this sincere? Did I assume they always had some ulterior motives just because I always did?

Lyndsay saw me coming and winked. Of course she knew where I'd been and what I'd been doing, she was one of my best friends. I thought back to Mr. Hughes- of the way I'd heard her sobs in my head while I made him scream. Was that what friendship was?

I could have gone on like that all night. I walked through a party like a hundred others I've been too and, for the first time, I had no idea where I was going.

I could always trust my instincts. That day in San Clemente, I had opened up the cellar of my brain and discovered that there were things living there that were never wrong. They were ugly and ill-mannered but they were always unquestionably trustworthy. With them to turn to, I never had to question if what I was doing was right. Kill when I wanted, kiss Anthony when I wanted, it was how I'd always lived and I'd never been led anywhere to make me doubt the wisdom of those voices.

But up until now those cellar creatures had always spoken in one voice. If the things that lived down there were always right, what was I supposed to do when they didn't agree?

The desire to kill would never go away. I knew that as surely as I knew I'd never stop loving Canadian bacon.

Or that I would never stop loving Anthony.

So stay with him. But kill someone first. *If you hurry back he'll never even know you left.* One of those solar-powered path lights will work. *If he's asleep you could wake him with a kiss.* If the stake's sharp enough to go into the ground it's sharp enough to go into flesh.

Neither voice would be silent. Each one assured me that it was right and if I listened to it I would never know a single moment's regret for the rest of my life.

But what could I do when each voice was telling me to kill the other one?

"Well, that took longer than I expected," a knowing voice said. "McLovin must have had even more in storage than I thought."

It was Alicia. Seeing her now just raised another question. Could I have made the play special just by being a good actress? Not even a Tony winner, but just good enough to get past people's cynicisms and low expectations and actually make them feel something? If I wasn't a murderer, JCH wouldn't have had a dead quarterback to canonize. Just being good might have been enough to put us ahead.

But would it have made me happy?

Alicia mistook my silence for something to do with her.

"I'm just being a bitch," she said. "You know I love you."

"I know." *But I didn't know until right now that I loved you too.*

"So what's the problem? Did it go alright? Anthony didn't get lost on the way down did he? Please tell me he didn't cry."

"It was great," I said. "Really." Because even if we were truly friends, I couldn't tell her what I was feeling. There were parts of my life that nobody could know about, especially not if I was thinking about abandoning them.

"Excellent," Alicia said with feigned sincerity. "It's too bad you already said you were only going to stay with him for the summer. You know, Caltech isn't THAT far from Santa Cruz. If he's as good in bed as you say, maybe I'll invite him up for a visit sometime."

My eyes flashed. "If you touch him, I'll-"

Cut your fucking hands off is what I was about to say. Fortunately for both of us, Alicia's laughter cut me off before I could finish.

"Got ya," she smirked.

"You're an evil bitch," I said.

Alicia held out her hands. "Hey, already said I was. But I am just repeating what you said. If any of it sounds evil or bitchy, then welcome to the club."

"You're the one that's been on me about dropping him. Don't make me feel bad about it or I might change my mind."

"Is that what you want to do?" she asked.

"Change my mind? No. The last thing I want to do is change my mind. I just- I just wish that leaving was still easy."

"Beverly, did you ever really think it was going to be easy? This is your whole life you're walking away from. Did you really think that there was nothing it would hurt to leave behind?"

"As someone I was planning to leave behind, is there a way for me to say 'yes' without offending you?"

"Not really, but us evil bitches have pretty thick skin." She considered the glum look on my face. "And it's hard to get offended when it looks like you're figuring out for yourself how not easy it's going to be. I'm actually kind of flattered."

"But I do want to go," I burst out. "I need to. If I stay here, all I'm ever going to be is my parent's daughter and your friend and Anthony's girlfriend. It's not enough. I want...."

I want to live for terror and glee and exhilaration. I want to see what blood looks like in fresh snow. I want to know if a Kukri knife can really decapitate someone in one swing. I want to know what it's like to live my life without anybody waiting for me to come home or text them back or pretend like I care about anything except murder.

"...I want to be more."

Alicia nodded but I could tell she didn't get it.

"So go," she said. Maybe she didn't understand, but there was no anger or condemnation in her voice either. "It's your life. Do what's going to make you happy. That's what they keep ramming down our throats. You're also a special snowflake, in case you didn't know."

"But I'd be happy if I stayed." The words came out before I could consider them, but they were true. I would genuinely and honestly be happy if I stayed with these people, this real family I'd drawn around myself without even realizing it. "I already am happy." The realization hit me like a hammer.

Alcia shrugged. "So stay."

"You're a real big help, Alicia."

The gentle smile never left her face. It looked weird on her, but it stayed right where it was.

"You don't need my help," she said. She set her drink down so she could grab my shoulders with both hands. She turned me to face her.

"Beverly Angela Kilbourne," she said. "You are a fucking shark. You wanted to be a varsity cheerleader when you were a sophomore? You did it. You decided you were going to make it facebook official with an absolute zero on the social scale? You did it. Not because anyone encouraged you or told you it would be a good idea, but because you know who you are in a way that most people never will."

She got up close so our noses were only inches apart. "Look me in the eye," she said. "Look me in the eye right now and tell me that you don't already know what it is that you want to do."

...I couldn't. Alicia had done for me what I couldn't do for myself. She cut through the swirling chaos of my surface thoughts so I could see the current of instinct running straight and true as ever.

It told me what I needed to do.

I smiled and my best friend smiled with me.

"Thank you, Alicia."

I hugged her and she rocked with the motion of it.

"You would've worked it out for yourself," she said, making no effort to remove herself from my arms. "I just helped you along so you wouldn't spend all summer on this 'will I or won't I' bullshit."

"Still. I love you."

"I love you too. No lesbo."

She looked over my shoulder. "Speaking of no lesbo, look who's up and walking like a man."

I turned. It was Anthony. He looked anxious, obviously thinking of all the reasons it could be bad that he woke up and I wasn't there.

"I should go talk to him," I said.

"Go," Alicia said warmly. "But keep this Wonder Years moment between us girls, ok?"

"Don't want anyone to know the ultimate bitch is going soft?" I teased.

She pinched some nonexistent flab. "I'm going soft all over."

I reached into my purse for something I'd thought about giving her all night. I was worried it might be the wrong decision, but now it finally seemed right to give it to her.

"Here," I said and handed over a sample packet of pills. "New diet pills my mom's company's been working on. Not to be taken with alcohol so don't use them tonight." I smiled. "My graduation gift to you... and my way of telling you how much you mean to me."

"Thanks, Bev." Her voice was casual but I noted the way she almost snatched the pills from me. Still, she pocketed them and picked up her drink. There weren't any warning lights telling me that she would pop them the second my back was turned.

She waved her drink at me. "I'm going to find somebody cute and stupid to share this with. Find me later." And then she was gone.

Anthony lingered by the gazebo, trying to play it cool and not at all showcasing any of the acting talent I knew he had.

I walked towards him and realized just how perfect everything around us was. The air carried a faint hint of the ocean breeze from Santa Monica and it was tinged with the smell of good weed from by the pool. The sound of the party around us blended into a pleasant jumble of good feelings personified.

Most of all, there was the way Anthony looked in the dim lantern light. I slowed my pace so I could memorize the angles of his face. It was his eyes I wanted to hold onto the most. Nobody had ever looked at me the way Anthony did and I never felt more loved than when I was looking at him.

I went to him and took his hands in mine. "Hey."

"Hey," he said back. "Thought for a second there you'd ditched me," he joked and not joked.

I shook my head. "No." I kissed him. "Never."

47

My mom was crying. Ever since my hospital stay, she cried more, smiled more, and laughed more. The only thing she did less was stay at the office.

My dad squeezed her knee. He was misty-eyed too. "I know," he said.

We were on our way to graduation. My dad was driving, probably for the best since my mom burst into tears every time she looked in the rearview mirror and saw me in my cap and gown.

"I just can't believe it's really you," she bawled. "You look so mature."

I rolled my eyes. "Ok, mom."

"Got your speech?" my dad asked.

I patted the hip pocket where my index card notes resided. "Right here," I said.

"You're going to kill 'em, honey," my dad said.

"It really is a great speech, Beverly," my mom gushed.

I'd spent a week working on it. I didn't know if it was great or not. The one thing I knew for sure was that it was honest.

We got to the ceremony a half hour early but the parking lot was already almost full. There were heavy streaks of green in the mix of colors working their way towards the football field, my fellow graduates in their robes.

I wondered how many other types of events could guarantee the kind of widespread good feelings that came with a graduation. I looked at the crowd around me and saw no frowns, no tears but those of joy. If there was fear of separation or change, today it was overshadowed by appreciation of the lives already lived and the relationships already made.

I looked and realized that there was one other event guaranteed to make people feel as good as the ones here.

A healthy birth.

An unblemished beginning of something new and full of potential.

"Beverly!"

Anthony ran toward me, his gown billowing behind his slight frame. He reached me and went in for the kiss. Then, at the last moment, he saw my dad get out of the car and turned it into an awkwardly angled hug. I would have taken it over a hundred kisses from anybody else.

Anthony turned towards my parents. "Hi, Mrs. Kilbourne," he said. He nodded dutifully at my dad. "Sir."

"Anthony," my dad returned noncommittally. He saw it as his duty to keep Anthony fearful and convinced he wasn't good enough, not that Anthony needed the help, but he'd also already told me how much he liked him. "Where are your parents?"

"Oh, they didn't want to come," he grinned. "Joking. They've already got their seats. I was just..."

"Waiting for me?" I finished with a smirk.

"Nooo," he drawled. But of course he was.

A sudden air horn blast kept me from interrogating him further. "ONE HOUR," Curtis bellowed. He loosed another deafening blast from the air horn. "ONE HOUR UNTIL WE'RE OFFICALLY LOOSE UPON AN UNSUSPECTING WORLD." He was coming toward us with Lyndsay by his side. Alicia followed them at a more leisurely pace, trying to pretend like she wasn't amused by Curtis' antics.

"You're not going to use that during the ceremony, are you?" I asked.

"No," Lyndsay cut in before Curtis could say anything. "He isn't." She side-eyed him in a way that reminded me of my mother. "Isn't that right, Curtis?"

He nodded emphatically. "Yes, ma'am. Or, no ma'am. Whichever's right."

My dad winced. "Oh, that is the wrong road to start down my young friend."

My mom elbowed him. He laughed and threw an arm around her.

I took Anthony's hand. "Let's go. If I'm late and you're late then they're going to give the speech to Lucy Benson."

"No chance," he squeezed my hand. "We'll get you there."

We started towards the student holding area when my mom called out.

"Wait," she yelled. She had her camera out. "One picture."

"Mommm," I groaned and hid my face behind my cap.

"Come on," my dad said. "One picture for your mother."

My friends were more accommodating. Lyndsay was already leaning forward and puckering her lips at the camera while Alicia angled her body towards what she thought of as her "thin side." I just threw both arms around Anthony while everyone crowded around us.

I didn't have to see his face to know how broadly he was smiling.

I didn't even have to look at the picture afterwards. I knew how happy we all were.

48

ANTHONY DIDN'T FIND me again until after my speech had been made, the diplomas had been handed out, and our mortarboard caps had been thrown into the air.

He came up behind me, weaving his way through the bustling, chatting crowd and kissed the side of my neck where he knew it would make me shiver. I sighed and pressed my body harder against his.

"Don't let my dad catch you doing that," I said.

"That's why I did it now," he said. His lips were still pressed against my skin. Every murmured syllable was a delicious caress. "That was a great speech, Beverly."

"It was alright."

"Joel Goodson's speech when he got caught stealing from the treasury was alright. THAT was fantastic."

Lyndsay and Alicia joined us. The mascara running down their faces was probably another vote for "great." Even Alicia was sobbing as they both hugged me.

"That was so good!" Alicia said.

I was starting to feel something damp at the corner of my eyes. "Come on, guys," I tried to slip out and they just hugged me harder.

"They're right," Curtis weighed in. "That was so good I'm glad Lyndsay took my air horn." He turned to his girlfriend. "Speaking of, can I have my air horn back?"

"No," Lyndsay said without taking her head out of my shoulder.

"All right," I finally said. "Come on, you guys are crushing me." I managed to slip out of their grasp while Alicia and Lyndsay sniffed and wiped their eyes.

"Pre-prom still at your house?" Alicia asked.

I nodded. "Five-thirty food. Seven-thirty limo."

"Plenty of time for pictures and appetizers," Curtis put in.

"Just leave some food for the rest of us," Anthony said.

"Relax, I'll leave some weenies for the weenie."

Curtis was going to school in Indiana. It wasn't hard to see how easy it would be for him and Anthony to stay close.

"I'll see you guys in a few," I said. We all started to drift back towards our respective families, to be cooed over and praised for God knows how long.

"Hey, guys?" Lyndsay called out.

We all turned. Lyndsay shuffled her foot, reluctant to continue.

".....We made it," she said.

The statement wasn't greeted by the easy smiles you'd expect. I didn't even know if it was true. Could it really be called "making it" if you couldn't even recognize who you were on the other side? Out of all of us, Alicia was the only one who was maybe even close to being the person she was when the year began. And even that might have been wrong because she certainly seemed as perturbed as any of us when she finally spoke.

"Yeah. I'll.... I'll see you guys tonight."

Lyndsay nodded. "For sure." Whatever conclusions she'd drawn, she certainly seemed happy with them.

We separated.

FINAL INTERLUDE:

THE GRADUATION SPEECH

- - -

Beverly walks up to the podium. The principal has already spoken. The guest speaker, a moderately successful TV writer and alumni, has already spoken. Now, the stage is hers. She looks out over the crowd. Four hundred classmates and easily twice as many parents, siblings, relatives, step-siblings, step-parents, and single parents.

She is not afraid. Beverly opens her mouth and her voice rings out strong and true.

"My fellow graduates..."

- - -

Lyndsay is the first one to arrive at the house.

She's wearing her hair up with only a few tantalizing strands cascading down to frame her face. Her dress is canary yellow. A one-of-a-kind masterpiece that she had custom made months in advance. It clings tightly to her every curve and the strapless bodice is cut so deeply through the cleavage that it's miraculous it's able to stay up. She'd planned to wear it for Mr. Hughes but she's glad that Curtis will get to see her in (and out) of it instead.

Beverly's mother answers the door. Tina lays eyes on Lyndsay, a girl whose pigtails she once braided, and is struck forcefully by just how far gone those days are.

Then, Lyndsay smiles at her and she sees so much of the same cheerful, sweet-natured girl staring back at her that she realizes just how little all of that passed time really means.

"Hey, Mrs. Kilbourne."

Tina finally finds her voice again. "Oh, Lyndsay," she says. She raises her voice. "Jerry?! Come look at Lyndsay!"

Beverly's father enters from the kitchen. He stops dead and his eyes widen. He lets out a long wolf whistle. "Wow. Hubba, hubba."

"Jerry!" his wife cries out, scandalized and embarrassed.

He throws his hands up innocently. "What?" He makes a show of seeing Lyndsay for the first time. "Oh, hey, Lyndsay. You look nice too." He winks at his wife. They're like that now, flirting and teasing as if they were just starting to date. In a very real sense, that's exactly what they're doing.

"Where's Beverly?" Lyndsay asks.

"She'll be down in a minute," Jerry says. "She just got back from picking something up and now she's doing....," he shrugs, lost in a world of procedure and terminology more complicated than anything he learned as a cop, "something to her hair."

Tina rolls her eyes. "Why that girl didn't just get a stylist, I have no idea."

"That's Beverly," Lyndsay says. "Always has to do it her own way."

Tina smiles but it's a small crease only meant for herself, a moment's pride at the self-sufficient, capable young woman she's raised.

Then, a voice floats down the stairs, claiming all of their attention. "If you're all talking about me anyway, maybe somebody could tell me how I look?"

Except, they can't.

They are a police officer, a chief operating officer, and a C-student. There is not a poet among them. Even if there was, William Shakespeare would be at a loss to describe the vision coming down the stairs. A photographer could never successfully capture the energy and grace that flexes and emanates from her every step. A cinematographer shooting at 1080p would fumble on the slopes of her beauty and inevitably slip off of them.

All they can do is stare with something close to religious awe. Beverly is simply more stunning than anything any of them have ever known.

Her dress is pure white. Subtle hints of crystal woven into the fabric makes her shimmer with every step. Her long hair hangs simply over one shoulder in a cord of woven rose gold. Brightest of all are her eyes, her eyes that are so full and expressive. Even if everything else could be cast aside, there would be no speaking over her sapphire eyes.

Finally, Beverly snorts back a laugh. "Ok, take it easy. It's not like when I went upstairs I was wearing glasses and a head brace."

That doesn't break the spell but it does diminish it. Tina's able to lift her camera again. "You and Lyndsay get together," she says.

The girls comply. Despite their glamorous appearance, the girls put up piece signs and stick their tongues out at the camera. This is not a portrait photo to be hung as a conversation piece, this is a perfect moment to be captured in time. They've graduated high school happily and healthily. In less than an hour, young men that they love will escort them to an evening meant to celebrate that fact. Afterwards, they both have private bedrooms in a house in Malibu.

If the camera is not quite up to the task of capturing their beauty, it can at least convey their joy.

- - -

"Respected teachers," Beverly continues. "Treasured families. Welcome, and thank you for coming." She smiles. "Before we begin, I'd like to remind you that up until now every time I've had to motivate a football field full of

people, I 've had the distinct advantage of being able to do so in a short skirt." She lifts one gown-draped leg from behind the podium to laughter from the crowd along with a few good-natured wolf whistles. "So, I'll do my best but I hope you'll forgive me if my words aren't as inspiring as my back handsprings."

- - -

Her hair and makeup are done but Alicia still hasn't left her house. Her stylist was the same one that Scarlett Johansson used for the Oscars. Together, they decided on a pale, creamy motif that emphasizes Alicia's dark hair and makes her eyes glow like twin emeralds. Her dress is a Louis Vuitton original. It hugs her petite body and a long slit in the red dress showcases a length of very admirable leg.

Alicia looks at herself in the mirror and shakes her head in disgust.

She can't understand how it's possible. She's eaten nothing but half a rice cake a day for two weeks. How could she still be this bloated and revolting? It's a miracle her high heels don't snap beneath the weight of her lard-packed ass.

She turns from the mirror, trying not to cry because if she ruins her makeup she really will look like reality show trailer trash but she can't help it because it's all so UNFAIR. Lyndsay and Beverly never do anything except whatever fad diet's popular and they're both so skinny (except where they're not supposed to be) while she, Alicia, purges and starves herself and runs three miles every day and somehow still wakes up every morning with another roll of fat (except where she's supposed to have two). And, surprise, surprise, it's Beverly and Lyndsay who have dates while she has to pretend to be happy about going solo even though with everything she did to put this prom together you think somebody would have the fucking gratitude to...

Won't cry, she repeats. *Won't cry, won't cry, won't cry.* But she's biting her lip so hard against the tears that her blood starts to flow instead. Every drop dripping down her chin lands in her lap but they might as well be one crushing weight on her overburdened back after another until, finally, she collapses under the weight. Alicia's had enough. She's going to call Beverly and tell her she's not coming.

Her hand is on the phone when she remembers the pills.

She claws desperately through her purse. Prom's a lost cause, but if it kicks in overnight then just maybe she can still look halfway human in a bikini for the weekend.

She finds the pills. Her hands are trembling as she opens the sample packet. After-prom's more important anyway. By then, people care less about who they went with and are more interested in who they haven't had yet. The thought that for the first time in her life she's settling for being second best never crosses her mind.

The packet finally opens. She dry swallows both pills and closes her eyes. Like with most medication, the pills heal her mind before her body. She realizes she can paint her lips a darker shade of red and nobody will notice the cut. She hasn't ruined everything. It's all still under control.

She's reaching for the lipstick when the first stomach cramp hits her. She winces and clutches her stomach. It can't be menstrual. She's not due for another two weeks.

Then another one hits like a merciless wave. Alicia falls to her knees and moans. Her skin feels clammy and she's starting to sweat.

Another bolt of pain runs through her. Now there's no stopping the tears. She tries to call for help and can't through the agony. There's no space between the pains now. It's a living thing of razors, growing inside of her and cutting deeper and deeper with every passing second.

She vomits with concussive force. Not that there's much in her stomach but what little there is shoots from her mouth and spatters her hands. The strength runs from her limbs and she collapses into the puddle. *My dress,* she realizes. *I'm ruining my dress.*

She still can't get up. She vomits again and this time only clear, ropey strips of bile come out. They cling to her chin and suddenly dry lips and the scent assails her nostrils.

Alicia tries to crawl for the door, ignoring the pain as she's always ignored everything in her way, but the urge to vomit strikes her again and she has to stop. She retches uncontrollably and wonders, *What now?* Her body can't possibly have anything left to vomit out, no matter how hard her stomach's squeezing itself.

Then, her whole body convulses and a stream of blood jets from her throat.

Alicia's emerald eyes brighten with panic. She tries to clench her teeth and clamp a hand over her mouth but her whole body is in revolt. Her esophagus contracts and another flood burst of blood overflows past her hand.

She reels sideways, soaked in her own fluids. A sound escapes her, a primordial, frog-like gurgle that she's never made before, even when she, Beverly, and Lyndsay went to that frat party at Dekker University, and this time spongey, pink pieces of stomach lining come up along with the blood.

She collapses, too weak to move. She can feel her own viscera soaking into her hair and into her dress, irrevocably ruining everything.

Incredibly, Alicia feels good.

Truthfully, she feels thin. If she had the strength to stand and look in the mirror, and if she could clean the blood and vomit from her dress, she thinks she would look fantastic.

Her eyes flutter but she can't nap now. She has too much to do. She's already late for Beverly's and if she doesn't get moving she'll miss the prom entirely. And there's no way that's going to happen. Not when the Kincaids are going to be there. Not now after all the work she's put in.

She feels lighter still. She lets her head sink against the floor.

Ok, maybe just a quick nap and then I'll put myself back together again.

Her eyes close.

Alicia's lighter than air.

Somebody knocks at her door.

"Alicia, honey?"

Her mother opens the door. She's smiling as best she can with the moving parts of her face made rusty by one facelift too many.

"Can I get a photo with you before you leave?"

She sees her daughter.

At first, she's just frozen. The gears of her features grind and struggle through denial and botox to relay what she's feeling.

Then, the grease of fear finally seeps in, lubricating everything with horror and revulsion.

When it does, Alicia's mother finds her voice and screams out into the twilight.

- - -

When the laughter fades, Beverly grows serious again. "I didn't know what to expect when I came to high school. I don't think any of us did. Sure, maybe some of us felt like we ran the show in middle school, but we all knew this was a new game the second we walked through the doors. Like most of you, I didn't know where I was going to fit in. I didn't know who was going to like me.... and I didn't know that I was about to have the best four years of my life.

In the audience, the waterworks have begun. Lyndsay and Alicia are already wiping their eyes.

- - -

Beverly and Lyndsay go up to her room. Jerry follows them with Lyndsay's overnight bag. "There you go," he says and sets it down. "Safely out of the way of pictures until the limo gets here. You girls want to sneak some food before the rest of our esteemed guests arrive?"

There's a purple, tissue-filled bag at the foot of the bed. Carefully, Beverly toes it around the corner and out of sight. "In a second," she says casually to her father. "I want to talk to Lyndsay about something first."

Jerry tips them a wink as he goes. "Ah, girl talk. Say no more." He hasn't noticed Beverly's sleight of foot but Lyndsay has and she's struggling to hide a smile.

The second he's gone, Lyndsay dances to the far side of the bed and picks up the bag. "Could our girl talk have something to do with this?" She makes the bag dance from its handles like a marionette on strings. "Little something from Salma's Secrets for Anthony?" she teases.

"Maybe," Beverly says. She doesn't smile back. She wants Lyndsay to open it and she wants to be done with this.

Lyndsay doesn't notice the pall over Beverly's face. She's too busy pulling away the pink tissue paper. "Let's see. It's too heavy to be just lingerie. Maybe some-"

She pulls away the last of the tissue paper and there's no moment of shock before Lyndsay starts screaming. For all of her intellectual short comings, Lyndsay's heart processes things much faster than either Beverly's or Alicia's and she immediately starts to moan the second she sees Curtis' severed head staring back at her from inside the bag.

"No, no, no, no, no, NO, NO! NO! NO!" The rest is just ear-piercing howls of horror and pain but they're different than the cries of most people Beverly has killed. They come from some place deeper and more irreparably damaged than simple terror. Even if Lyndsay were to survive, she would spend the rest of her life as a hollow, broken person.

Beverly hasn't actually thought about it, but it's quite possible that that's why she chose to let her see Curtis the way she did.

Killing her now would be a mercy.

Lyndsay drops the bag. There's a dull thud when Curtis' head hits the ground. She turns and bolts for the door.

Beverly turns and goes into her underwear drawer.

She comes out with an enormous two-handed meat cleaver.

Lyndsay's hand is on the door when Beverly swings the cleaver into her back. Beverly aims high, severing the top of Lyndsay's spinal cord and wiping all pain from her body.

It's not like she wants Lyndsay to suffer.

Her screams are cut along with her spine. Lyndsay slumps against the door and Beverly works the cleaver out of bone. She can hear twin thunderheads already coming up the stairs and she pulls harder at the cleaver. She doesn't have much time.

"BEVERLY?! BEVERLY?!"

The thunder gets closer. Her parents. All they're thinking about is Lyndsay's screams. In their minds, if Lyndsay's in danger Beverly must be as well. They don't know what could be behind the door to make a young woman scream in such utter refusal and they don't care. All they know is the single biological imperative of protecting their child.

The door flies open, knocking aside the 125 pound deadweight of Lyndsay's body as if it were nothing. Jerry bursts in first with Tina close behind him. His trained eyes sweep the room, his body is tensed to protect the one thing he loves most.

He still never sees it coming as Beverly swings the bloody cleaver at his face.

— — —

"Our time here has been more perfect than we could ever have dreamed. We have had a safe harbor where we were free to realize our passions, hone our talents, and become the people that we were truly meant to be."

The crowd listens with more than mere politeness. None of them expected someone so young to speak with such force and conviction. And yet, she is and they are swept away by it.

"But now, the time has come to leave harbor and set sail out into the world. A world full of storms and hardships that will force you to compromise who you are if you want to be a part of it." She takes a deep breath, as if staring down this challenge for herself.

"...Don't let it."

— — —

She splits her father's head vertically down the middle.

She catches her mother in the hip, chopping through so many major arteries that her legs turn purple with pooled internal bleeding.

Curtis' head rolled out of the bag after Lyndsay dropped it and it has taken its place in the abattoir. If Lyndsay was still asphyxiating after her spine was cut, she's dead now. Her glassy eyes stare up at Beverly from the floor.

Somewhere, most likely in her own room, Alicia is dead too if Beverly knows her at all. And of course she does.

They're best friends.

- - -

"My classmates. My friends," she says with tears shimmering in her own eyes. "If we are truly capable of achieving anything we're willing to strive for, then our future is not a question of what we can do but of what we are willing to do without. With that in mind, I implore you to never compromise. Do whatever it takes to make sure that your essential self is your only self. And make no mistake, you will be tempted. Good things will be put in front of you."

She looks at her parents. Her friends.

Anthony.

"Wonderful things that can be yours if you're only willing to put aside the person that you know you were meant to be and become who you're expected to be."

She fights to keep her voice even but everyone can hear the emotion boiling behind it. In the years to come, her fellow graduates will remember her words as they deliberate over job prospects and personal choices. Many of them will hear Beverly's voice as they choose what will make them happy over what will make them rich.

"But, as much as you may want to, don't accept them. Instead, choose a life where you can wake up every morning and say, 'I know I am doing what I was put on this earth to do and I CANNOT and WILL NOT be made into anything else...'"

49

BEVERLY

"NO MATTER THE COST."

That's how the speech ended. "I will not be made into anything else, no matter the cost."

I let the cleaver slip from my hand. It hit the ground without making a whisper. The carpet was too soaked with blood for it to make any noise. The walls were drenched too. My dress wasn't white anymore, it was soaked red with cost.

Looking at them all, I felt no remorse. Nagging sorrow? Yes, but not regret.

I'd done the only thing I could do.

I was right from the beginning, you see. I was a killer. Underneath anything else I could be: daughter, friend, lover, I was first and foremost always a murderer.

Ladies and Gentlemen, let's welcome Steve Harvey to the stage.

I thought that was supposed to be my line.

Not this time, Steve. Tonight, you're the contestant. Does that sound alright?

I told you before, Beverly. You're the one running this show. We can do whatever you want.

Alright then. In that case, let's move on to our first category. Now, there are seven answers on the board and, like you said, this is my game. So, instead of being allowed three wrong answers, you don't get any. You make a single wrong guess and I cut your head off. Sound fair?

Can't say it does. But I can't say that I have a choice either, can I, Bev?

No, you can't. So make your first guess.

I'd be happy to but you seem to have forgotten to tell me the category.

Steve, I'm disappointed. You already know the category. The category is.... What Would Make Beverly the Happiest for the Rest of Her Life. Now make your fucking guesses.

Alright, Bev. I'm going to say, "Buying your parents a card for their anniversary and feeling like they'd actually be happy to get it."

Not bad. That's answer number seven. You're on the board.

Still got a lot of blanks to fill. How about, "Hanging out at the beach with Lyndsay between classes?"

Another excellent choice. Number six answer.

"You and Lyndsay telling Alicia that you love her and you want her to get help... and hearing her actually agree to get treatment?"

Number five.

Is, "The shudders of a dying man with a power drill on his stomach," up there?

You know it is. Answer number four.

Getting tricky now, but could the next one be, "finally getting a shark hook down someone's throat and yanking their tonsils out in one complete set?"

That's correct. You know what that means. Top three, Steve. You're in the top three. What's your pick for the number two thing to make me happiest?

That one's easy. Anthony.

You don't want to be more specific than that? Maybe, "Catching a before noon movie where the tickets are six dollars and there's nobody there to get annoyed if you talk and laugh as loud as you want?" Or maybe, "Reaching out after making love and feeling the warmth of his calf with my toes?"

No. That doesn't seem necessary. Just Anthony.

...Good answer, Steve.

Also the hardest one. If Anthony's the number two answer, then I know what's the number one thing that will make you happiest of all.

Well, don't keep us in suspense.

Going to New York.

Wrong answer. I don't give a shit about New York anymore. It's just a place and I know now that home is where your heart is. I know now that even if I left LA forever, I was always going to carry Alicia, Lyndsay, Curtis, and my parents around with me in my heart. So, the thing that would really make me the happiest is knowing that I'm not torn in half anymore. What I want more than anything else is to not have to choose between my bloodlust and my family.

Then why-

Because I can't love people who are dead.

Beverly-

I silenced the voice and then there was nothing.

I was alone with my dead.

And then someone was knocking on the door downstairs. It could only be one person.

I went downstairs to let Anthony in.

50

I DIDN'T PICK the meat cleaver back up. I already had a folding knife hidden in the cleavage of my dress.

It was a knife I was saving special for him.

I walked out of my room. Blood bubbled from the soaked carpet as my shoes squished through it.

My parents' bodies blocked the doorway. I had to step over them to get out.

Anthony knocked again. I didn't call out to him.

I was walking slowly. I kept waiting to feel some kind of delayed reaction to what I'd done. So far, I felt the same but I no longer trusted the thinkers in the cellar. I knew this was the right decision, but I was still on alert just in case some part of me rose up... I don't know, to defend him somehow.

If it did, I was ready to butcher it the second it appeared. I was done letting any other voices talk.

But it seemed like there was no objection from the cellar of my thoughts or anywhere else. There was no resistance, I felt nothing trying to stop me as I made bloody heel prints down the stairs. There was only the same rueful acceptance I'd felt when I took the knife to everyone else I loved.

The stairs weren't that far from the foyer. I crossed the living room in only three steps. I preferred walking on the carpet. My heels clicked across the stone floor and echoed through the house like it was a tomb.

Which of course, it was.

I reached the door and slipped the knife from my dress. I flipped it open. The blade was pristine silver, I'd never used it before so I took a moment to make sure my fingers fit securely into the grips.

I looked at the door in front of me and gauged Anthony's height against it. I was going to open the door and take him by surprise. Stab him through the eye and kill him before he had a chance to feel any pain.

I hesitated. I realized that I couldn't be sure if Anthony was standing directly in front of the door. What if he was slightly to the right or the left? If my aim was off, then I might just take off an ear or cut a gash into his skull. If I missed then I would have to stab him again and he would see the killing blow coming. He would be-

I'm not going to miss, I swore. My grip on the knife tightened. I looked at the door again and saw with cool certainty where I was going to put the knife. And if it looked like I was going to miss, then I could adjust mid stab and rip open an artery instead. He would still be dead before he knew what was happening.

The preparation was done. I lifted my free hand and felt the curve of the doorknob beneath my palm. I took a cleansing breath, the kind of thing Alicia always told us to do before going on stage, and raised the knife.

It was showtime.

The knife moved first. When I flung the door open, the blade would already be halfway towards Anthony's eye.

And then the revolt came. I had no chance of stopping it because it was from the last place I expected.

It was the knife that refused to obey. Instead of flying straight for Anthony's face, it dove and plunged deep into my other hand before I could open the door. I drove the blade through my own flesh until it hit bone.

The only reason I didn't scream was because I knew if Anthony heard it, he would come rushing inside.

To protect me.

The blade felt like fire going in. It should have hurt even more going out but I barely felt it. All I felt was sick to my soul.

I clutched my hand and sunk to my knees. Blood was pooling on the tile floor. I could see my reflection in it and there was no agony looking back at me, only revulsion.

This is true love, I realized dimly. This rotten ache in my soul that made my gouged hand feel like a pinprick, this was love. Even now, all I wanted to do was open the door, throw my gore-streaked arms around him, and let him taste somebody else's blood on my lips.

Instead, I bit my lip until I broke skin and more of my blood flowed.

Let it. Everyone else had to put some into the pot. Why shouldn't you?

I rocked back and forth on my knees, cradling my gouged hand until the bleeding slowed and my heart stopped screaming.

I couldn't kill him.

I was going to have to hurt him.

Anthony, I'm so sorry.

51

THE FIRST THING TO do was bandage my hand. It wasn't easy, the knife had damaged a nerve and my ring finger wasn't working properly anymore.

When it was done, I stripped out of my dress and washed the blood from my face and arms. Then, I went down to the laundry room and threw on the first clean set of clothes I could find.

I went back upstairs. My dad's wallet was on the counter. He was a cash only kind of guy and he and my mom had been planning to go on a weekend trip while I was in Malibu. I opened his wallet and pocketed the two thousand dollars I found inside.

My phone was on the counter next to my dad's wallet. It started to ring.

I checked the caller ID:

ANTHONY <3

It didn't surprise me that he'd waited on the doorstep so long before calling. Hadn't he always been waiting for me?

I let it ring and looked at myself in the reflective chrome of the refrigerator.

When I'd cleaned the blood from my face, I'd wiped away all of my makeup along with it. The clothes I'd grabbed without thinking were faded jean shorts and an old t-shirt I had for lounging around the house. In Beverly Hills, you wouldn't even go out jogging dressed like this.

That was fine. I wasn't going to be in Beverly Hills much longer.

I had the money in one pocket. I had the folding knife tucked in the other.

It was everything I needed.

Or, at least, it would have been if I could have stacked Anthony's body alongside Curtis' head in my room.

Now, I would need my mother.

And I would need my phone.

And I guess I would still need the meat cleaver after all.

52

ANTHONY

HER PHONE WENT STRAIGHT to voicemail. I closed my eyes and listened to the music of her voice. "Hey, it's Beverly. If you're hearing this, it means I'm doing one of, like, a million different things so take your pick. But, leave a message if you want and I'll call you back when I'm not so busy."

I waited for the beep. Stupid really, unless you had a specific message nobody really bothered with voicemails anymore. You either sent a text or you waited for the person to see they had a missed call and called you back. I always left Beverly voice messages anyway. She'd inevitably listen to them like four days later and I'd always get some smart ass text in return. The fun part was I never knew when I'd get them. It was like pre-ordering a surprise smile for myself.

"Hey, Bev," I said. "I'm out front. Hoping you didn't decide to leave me in the most soul crushing way possible." I laughed. "Let me in."

A thousand years ago, by this point I would have counted every miserable way that her not answering for this long could lead to heart-wrenching humiliation that I would never recover from.

Now, I knew better.

I knew that she loved me.

And, sure enough. My phone buzzed a second after I hung up.

"Are you downstairs?"

"Yeah," I texted back.

"Give me 10 mins. No1 else is here and I'm still getting dressed."

I smiled. "Nobody there, huh? Not dressed, huh?"

"Perv," She sent back. "Relax. We've got all weekend ;)"

All weekend.

My God. I would have waited my whole life for an hour. Now, I just had to wait ten minutes for a whole weekend. I lost my balance, and not because I tripped. I let my weight rest against the door and laughed with sheer amazement at just how incredible my life was.

It was weird though, because I could have sworn that I'd pulled up behind Lyndsay's convertible when I got here.

So you found two BMW convertibles that looked alike? Do you want to call the newspapers?

I shook my head. I couldn't even pick on myself without smiling. I didn't see Alicia or Curtis' cars either. No surprise, Curtis was late to just about everything. And, according to Beverly, Alicia would fuss with her makeup for at least another twenty minutes before she showed.

With nothing else to do, I craned my head to see if I could get a peek at Mr. Kilbourne's new Stingray, but no luck. Him and Mrs. K were both pretty good about keeping their cars garaged.

So, I counted minutes. Minutes and fantasies.

9 minutes....

Beverly floating down the stairs in her prom dress.

7 minutes...

Beverly, walking down the aisle in a wedding dress.

5 minutes...

Beverly, sitting up in a hospital gown, cradling a newborn little girl who already had a thick crop of blonde hair.

3 minutes...

The garage next door opened. Beverly's neighbor, Mrs. Something, pulled out. Bev had told me about her. Mrs. Something was the widow of the Executive Vice President of Something. She had also taken on Beverly as a surrogate granddaughter. I'd already been warned that she was going to make an appearance before the limo arrived and that I should expect to hear plenty about how handsome I was and how her husband had escorted her to her own prom forty years ago.

All of that sounded fine by me.

Assuming, of course, that Mrs. Something would be back in time. I watched her pull out of her garage and turn down the street away from me in her nice, new Cadillac. Before she turned away from me, I also caught a glimpse of thick brown hair. Probably a dye job, but so what? It was a beautiful May day.

If it made her feel alive, that was what mattered.

53

BEVERLY

MY MOM WAS WAY LIGHTER than Mr. Hughes.

I was able to get her out of the house and into Mrs. Fey's back-yard in only two trips.

Old Mrs. Fey, naturally, had no objections to me breaking through the hedge wall between our yards with first one and then two sagging duffel bags. After all, Mrs. Fey had been stuffed into a rolling suitcase since six that morning.

I'd broken out the titanium hammer for that. It had turned her fragile skull to powder with one shot and very little blood. That was a relief; no need for cleanup then and no time for it now as I hurried out to the garage and got ready to leave. I had more bags than I expected, but the caddy was a big car. The two bags of mom fit nicely in the trunk along with the roller bag full of Mrs. Fey.

The car would have to go eventually. Not in Nevada, but maybe in Utah or even Colorado. I would need to keep my eyes open for someplace really remote. Somewhere that the car, and the bodies, would go undiscovered for at least a year.

That was an annoyance. A wrinkle I hadn't planned on. I'd hoped to get at least halfway across the country before having to switch cars. Mrs. Fey had no kids and no relatives. She could have been missing for days before anyone thought to look for her.

But, as I'd already learned, things changed.

The plan was supposed to be that, with my parents away and all of us going out, I would have had all of prom weekend to put distance between myself and anyone asking questions.

But Anthony was probably asking questions already. And with me, Lyndsay, Alicia, and Curtis not answering our phones, the only person he could ask was the police.

I could have still bought myself some more time. I could have texted him that it was over. That the last few months had been a big joke and the punchline was him waiting on my doorstep with a corsage I'd never wear in a million years. He would have left the house and I could have been in Alaska before he'd recovered enough to talk to his mother, never mind the cops.

It would have been easier for me to stab him in the heart.

I made it out into the Valley and didn't stop. There was no time for food. No time for hair dye. I pushed the wig more comfortably up on my head, not that I thought it would ever really be comfortable, and kept driving.

To distract myself, I started thinking about what I wanted my new name to be. Pamela maybe. Pam. That sounded like fun.

Please. Please, let it be fun.

Let Pam be smart. Let her always have just a little more money than she needs. Let her look good as a brunette. Let her wake up every morning and be satisfied with exactly where she is and what she's doing.

Let her be content. Let her be fulfilled. Let her enjoy winter.

Let her walk in dark alleyways and let the moonlight catch her smile.

Just don't let her be lonely. Don't let her feel empty.

Don't let her have regrets.

54

ANTHONY

I LOOKED at my phone while I waited for whatever happened next. I think someone said something about my parents coming to get me. I hadn't really been paying attention.

Prom was in full swing. My Instagram was drowning in photographs and hashtags.

#Kincaids.

#Prom

#Bffs.

#bestnight.

#PROM

#REM4LIFE

#loveyouall

#PROM!

None of them knew. They were singing along to Kincaids songs and drinking smuggled Vodka from water bottles without a care in the world. If anyone asked where Beverly, Lyndsay, or even I was, they didn't bother to wait for an answer. They were too busy dancing and eating and screaming themselves hoarse just to scream about what an amazing time they were having. It almost made you wonder why they were taking so many pictures of a night they'd never forget.

It was a night I'd never forget either.

Breaking through the back door of Beverly's house after fifteen minutes of unanswered calls and texts, terrified that she'd tripped and cracked her skull on her nightstand. Or maybe dropped her hair dryer in the bath tub.

Going upstairs. Discovering why Curtis and Lyndsay hadn't been answering me either.

#Mybffisdead

#blood

#screaming

#throwingup

#SCREAMING

#sirens

#crying

#SCREAMING!

The police questioned me back at the station. They said I could wait for a parent or a lawyer but they made it clear I wasn't a suspect and they just wanted to ask me some questions that might help explain what had happened. As if I cared about what happened to me anymore.

So, I talked.

They asked about our plans. When were people expected? Who knew we were going to meet at Beverly's house? Did Beverly have any enemies? They asked some questions about Lyndsay and Curtis too.

And they asked about Alicia, who wasn't even there. "Just background," they said. But, once or twice, the detective doing the interview slipped and referred to Alicia in the past tense.

I like to think of myself as pretty smart. I didn't need a multiple choice to know what it meant when Alicia was getting called a "was."

They also asked a lot of questions about Mrs. Kilbourne. A LOT of questions about Mrs. Kilbourne. Whether she'd seemed stressed.

If she approved of me. If she had a good relationship with Mr. Kilbourne. If she had a temper.

I didn't need to be smart to figure out why they'd be curious about Mrs. Kilbourne.

I'd seen the bodies. I knew who was lying there, chopped to pieces, *pieces*, and who wasn't.

Mrs. Kilbourne wasn't there.

And Beverly wasn't there.

But they used "was" when they talked about Beverly. And they used "is" when they were talking about her mother.

They were wrong. I didn't care what "evidence" they thought they had. Beverly wasn't dead. She wasn't. Her mother had left the other bodies behind. Why would she take Beverly with her if she'd killed her?

They think she's dead for the same reason you do. They didn't see the body but they saw the dress. That beautiful, white dress that was drenched with blood. You think a living person got pulled out of that thing? Her mother took the body for the same reason she sent you that text. Because she lost her fucking mind. They're going to find Beverly's body somewhere. They're going to find her naked in a ditch with mud in her hair and her throat-

SHUT UP! I didn't know that. I didn't know anything except that I loved Beverly. I loved Beverly and she loved me and-

The universe might be on your side, buddy.

That was right. The universe was on my side.

I laughed. I think it was a laugh. It might have been a sob.

Then, a warm hand fell on my shoulder. Not the universe. Just my dad. My mom was waiting in the car. They were here to get me. They said they would take me home and we would figure everything out together.

I'm not sure what they thought we needed to figure out, I knew exactly what I was going to do now.

I was going to wait for her.

I'd done it once before; I could do it again.

I would wait.

I would wait until Beverly found me again.

My dad guided me towards the door. We brushed past two cops talking to each other. One of them said something about a "-dilac."

I barely heard them. I was thinking about the beginnings of a song. The kind of thing my character from *Lofts* would write.

I'll leave the table set for two,

The left side of the bed, I'll save for you.

Beverly, no matter what I do,

My love for you will always stay true.

I would need a guitar. I felt my wallet bulging with my share of a limo and a beach house that no one was ever going to collect. I'd pick something up tomorrow.

And I'd get a tattoo with whatever was left. Beverly's face, tattooed right over my heart. That way I could see her in the mirror every morning before I got dressed.

It would do until she came back. And I knew, deep in my soul, that she would come back.

Or, maybe she wouldn't.

Maybe, this time, I would come to her.

BONUS STORIES

READ ON FOR THE BONUS SHORT STORY, "DON'T FEED THE ANIMALS."

DON'T FEED THE ANIMALS

Lacey didn't have a new boyfriend in mind when she broke up with Pat, but she knew exactly who her next boyfriend WOULDN'T be.

He would not belch or fart without warning. He would not drive a Honda Civic that always rattled like it was falling apart if it went past second gear. And, most of all, he would not always come up a little short for the dinner bill and a lot short in the bedroom.

Not that Lacey was exactly reaching for the stars, but she knew she could do better. And, as she settled into the leather seat of Harry's pickup truck, she realized she was right.

Leather in a pickup, she marveled. That said class. The gold card he'd paid for dinner with (NOT at a chain restaurant or a diner, thank you, God) said means. The broad shoulders and the gym bag she spied in the truck bed? That promised nothing but endurance in the bedroom.

If they even made it to an actual bedroom. The road they were on was without streetlights. There were no houses on either side of them, only the shadows of the trees whizzing by.

Harry wouldn't say where they were going, but Lacey was a local girl and she knew where they were going.

He was taking her to the lake.

And Lacey was just fine with that. If he wanted to, she'd fuck him right there on the shore. She'd sit him on a log and then she'd sit on his log and she'd ride him until one of those logs broke in half.

Her musings were interrupted as Harry pulled onto the side of the road and set the truck in park. "Here we are," he said, dazzling her again with that grin that had hooked her as she was getting off shift at the convenience store and reeled her in for a three course meal and then this winding drive through the high country.

"Here?" she asked. But she asked in a way that let him know she was still hooked and just fine to be reeled where ever he wanted.

Harry didn't answer. He just turned off the engine and stepped out of the truck. Lacey followed. She opened the door and the four cosmos she had with dinner (she'd ordered them with ice, real sophisticated-like) caught up with her. She slipped gracelessly from the truck and took four large, stumbling steps, giggling as she careened forward. She might have kept going, but Harry was there to catch her like the true gentleman he was.

"I almost broke my fucking neck!"she brayed in a very lady-like manner.

Harry kept her steady. "Easy, I've got you," he assured her. When he felt like she was balanced, Harry led her down the gentle incline away from the road and deeper into the woods. "Come on, we'll go nice and slow."

Not for long, we won't, Lacey thought. His touch was electric. Every one of his fingertips ran a charge through her skin and down into the nest of her lower belly. The charge was building between them and it was going to explode sooner, not later. She peered into the shadows of his face, trying to catch a glimpse of his amazing grey eyes. She couldn't, but she was able to catch the shift in the shape of his face. A smile.

"See?" he said. "Nothing to worry about."

"Just Korrigan?" she teased.

"That's right," he played along. "Just Korrigan, the Tombely's Lake monster who actually lives in the forest instead of the lake."

They both laughed. Lacey stumbled but Harry was there to catch her again. He wound up holding her up against a tree. They stayed like that for a moment against the tree trunk. Kissing close. Lacey felt his breath hot against her lips. Slowly, Harry went in for the kiss.

Lacey skirted away from him before his lips could touch hers. She would kiss him before the night was over, kiss him and take him twice around the world backwards, but that didn't mean she had to start the ride now. Where was the fun in that?

She took him by the hand and led him deeper into the woods. It had started as a whim, but now that she was out here, tasting the night air, she sincerely wanted to make love to him in view of the moonlight glistening on the lake.

"You know, my cousin's friend saw it once," she said.

"Korrigan?"

"Mhm." This was a stupid story, but it would work as a distraction until she wanted Harry to really focus on her. "He was fishing with baby ducks."

"For bait?!"

Lacey was pleased by his revulsion. She liked knowing something that he didn't. It made her seem more interesting.

"Big bait for big fish," she said.

"That's sick."

"Do you want to hear the story or not?"

"By all means, continue."

"Wellll, if you're sure. He was fishing in a little dinghy and he saw it running by the shore. He showed us pictures he took with his phone. This was like five years ago so the quality's bad but you can still totally see it."

"That's so amazing," he said.

"I know, isn't it crazy that we live right next to it?"

"No," Harry said. "I mean my uncle's stepdaughter's dentist has the same story. Only she saw Korrigan giving Bigfoot a reach around."

Lacey tried to swat him. Harry danced away, laughing as she

kept after him. Lacey was not so annoyed or amused to notice how easy he was on his feet. He probably did boxing or MMA. God, the body he must have under that shirt.

Their mating dance finally took them to the lakeshore. Lacey and Harry laughed and chased each other across the sand and it was exactly as romantic and perfect as Lacey thought. She slowed her pursuit to a jog. Sensing the game was moving to the next level, Harry slowed and turned to face her. She stepped in close to him and he wrapped his arms around her, molding her soft curves to the chiseled planes of his body.

"I was being serious," she said. As if she cared at all about whether or not some local urban legend existed right now.

"I'm sure," Harry said. His hands were moving on her back, slowly sliding above her pant line towards her front and leaving tingling trails in their wake. "But all I see is a beautiful view and a beautiful girl."

"No monsters?" she asked playfully. This time, she was the one leaning in.

His lips stopped just short of hers. "Oh, I don't know about that," he whispered.

"What do you mean?" she asked. But his hands were going to his belt. Jesus, if "Monster" was his name for it, she prayed fervently for truth in advertising.

And then the knife was in her stomach, sinking in through the flesh just over her belly button.

Lacey gasped. She looked down at the handle of the blade protruding from her stomach. Curiously, she could feel the whole length of the blade in her flesh but there was no pain that came with it. It was like the knife was a lightening rod, a homing beacon for all of the electricity that Harry's touch had been storing in her body. She could feel it all running back out and what was left was oh so cold and dead. Her limbs already felt cold and drained.

She looked up to Harry, as if he could have some explanation for this, but all she could see was his smile. It was wider now, and somehow more genuine, but it looked like he had more teeth. So many teeth...

He yanked the knife out of her gut. Lacey collapsed as if it had been her legs he'd cut and not her torso. She wheezed for breath, knowing that her life was leaving her with each exhale and she was powerless to do anything to stop it.

Harry waited and watched and listened. When he was sure Lacey was not just dying but actually dead, the man whose name was actually not Harry but Charlie tucked the knife back into his belt and started back towards his truck.

He whistled as he went.

He took his time walking back. Things had gone too well for him to ruin everything with a twisted ankle now. For such a local fixture, the lake was much more isolated than the quarry or the drainage ditches bordering the highway. It was very possible he had a real winner here.

His truck was right where he left it. Charlie went to the truck bed and opened the large gym bag. Inside the bag, there were several cinder blocks and lengths of chain. He grabbed a chain and a cinder block. Then, after considering the thighs on the dead woman and the extra serving of calamari she'd put away with dinner, he grabbed a second concrete block.

Lacey had misjudged Charlie on many levels, but her evaluation of his physical conditioning was dead on. He threaded the chain through both blocks and hefted them easily over one shoulder.

The way back to the lake was even easier than the walk there. His night vision was adapting and he was already feeling comfortable with the path from his truck to the lake. Not that he could do this once a week, no dump sight was that fool-proof, but all in all he was feeling as fine as a football fan on a Sunday afternoon.

When he got back to the shore and found the woman's body gone, his first reaction was not concern but confusion. Like a man who flipped on the TV and discovered kickoff had been preempted by the Yorkshire Dog Show.

He told himself he just didn't know the area as well as he thought he did. He'd moved at a wrong angle somewhere and had broken through the tree-line either too far east or west of where he'd left her. It never occurred to him that his date might have run out on him. He'd killed enough women to know when one was well and truly dead.

He looked to his right and didn't see her. He looked to his left and, sure enough, there she was.

She was being dragged towards the trees by Korrigan, the Tombely's Lake Monster who actually lived in the forest and not the lake.

It didn't look anything at all like it did on the gas station tee-shirts and books in the tourist shops. Those creatures always looked like a kind of off-model Bigfoot. Sometimes brown, sometimes black, but always shambling and burly looking. Even the skeptics dismissed "the creature" as an unusually large grizzly bear.

The thing dragging Lacey's body wasn't that big. It was larger than a bobcat but maybe five feet tall at the most. It's limbs were exceedingly long, like those of an orangutan. And strong, it was hauling better than a hundred and fifty pounds of dead Lacey as if it weighed no more than a dead mouse in the jaws of a cat. Its color was different too. The moonlight made it tricky, but Charlie would have pegged its fur as an old-chalk white or gray like dirty snow.

Oh, and, by the way, Charlie. Are you terrified right now?

Yes, he realized numbly. *I do believe I'm more scared than I've ever been in my life.*

Fear rooted him to the spot. The creature was moving away from him, at least there was that. But the body. What did it want with the body?

Well, that should have been obvious. And if it wasn't, Korrigan helpfully dipped its head down to rip a tasty morsel out of Lacey's left breast.

The block and chain slipped from his fingers. It narrowly missed fracturing his heel and hit the ground with a loud thump.

This is my wakeup call, Charlie thought as he felt the block fall.

Except he heard it hit and he didn't wake up.

Korrigan heard it and looked right at him. Its chin was dark with Lacey's blood.

Charlie ran.

There was no whistling or careful steps on his mad dash back to his truck.

- - -

He made it home going better than ninety-five without wrapping his truck around a telephone pole. He ran up his front steps without breaking his neck.

It wasn't until he was safely in his own bedroom, with the front door and the windows locked, that he started to really think about what he'd seen.

And about the corpse he hadn't quite disposed of properly.

- - -

He didn't get to sleep at all that night.

He stayed up in his office chair, smoking cigarettes and watching the horizon change from black to blue to rose orange. When his alarm went off at six o'clock, he was there to snap it off promptly. He stubbed out his last cigarette and went to the closet where he kept his work clothes.

He'd gone to the dry cleaner's the day before, and the Deputy's uniform was crisp and wrapped in plastic, exactly as he'd left it.

- - -

When he got to the station, Charlie went for the most haggard looking officer he could find. That happened to be Brad Waters, who always looked more than a little surly but seemed particularly displeased this morning.

"Waters," Charlie boomed in a boisterous tone that didn't reveal any hint of the anxiety he was feeling. It certainly didn't betray the way he was fingering the truck keys in his pocket as he approached the other officer. "Coming or going?"

Waters scowled without looking up from the paperwork he was filling out. "Going, thank God."

"Rough night?" Charlie asked. But he was beginning to hope maybe not *that* rough. Not with the casual way Waters was moving through his report.

"Only one call, but of course it was out to Lake PITA." Lake Pain in the Ass, the cop colloquialism for Tombely's Forest. Like any place where something paranormal was supposed to call home, the forest was a beacon for crank calls, mysterious disturbances, and most of all, false alarms.

"I'm guessing there was nothing to see," Charlie said.

"What do you think?" Waters asked. Charlie actually thought that there was a chewed over dead body and a low slung freak of nature with fangs and an appetite for human flesh to see, but he wanted to hear Waters thoughts, not his own.

"I didn't see anything. Including the pile of deer shit I stepped in during my thorough investigation of the area," Waters groused and held up the pink flimsy paper he was writing on. "I might as well just write 'drunk asshole' across this thing in huge block letters."

He may be an asshole, but Charlie hadn't been drunk when he made the call about the "strange figure" moving around Tombely's Forest. He had been driven by a clarity of terror that demanded he take a calculated risk to get ahead of this situation before it caught him unprepared.

Now, it was a different clarity, a clarity of excitement, that seized his mind as he went to his desk. He'd come into the station ready to take some "vacation time" at a moment's notice if anything felt even slightly wrong. But it would seem that the creature had been very diligent about cleaning its plate.

Extremely diligent.

- - -

Charlie had been watching the body for an hour.

He was far back from it, monitoring the corpse through the ghastly green glow of night vision goggles.

He'd killed the teen neatly with a single thrust through the underside of the jaw and into the brain, but when he spilled the body out onto the lake sand, he really *spilled* it. He'd cut open the boy's wrists and let the blood pool around him. He'd carved up the teenager's torso, exposing his organs, and took extra care to puncture the liver so the scent of the juices would filter out. He'd read somewhere that liver was like filet mignon to most predators.

All of that time and care and, still, nothing.

Another hour passed before he finally decided to just get rid of the body himself. He'd half-risen from his crouched hiding spot when the brush at the edge of the sand *coalesced* into a shape. Charlie quickly dropped back down. His heart was pounding. He'd been staring at that exact spot and hadn't noticed even a single rustling branch before the creature was suddenly loping across the sand in plain sight. Through the night vision goggles, he could see the creature more clearly than he had last night. The ripple of its muscles, the uncanny grace of its movements, and, last but very much not least, the curved claws and fangs that were too large for its mouth. They crowded past its lips and interlocked at crooked angles like barbed wire gates of hell.

Though the night was warm, Charlie suddenly felt cold. He fumbled for his pistol grip the way a frightened child would grab for his teddy bear.

He watched the creature sniff around the body and looked for even the slightest sign that it knew he was there. If it did, he would unload on it. Not cop style. Not measured shots with a breath between each one to re-center on your target. Most gift shops sold a Korrigan-themed pasta-strainer and Charlie would keep firing at it until life imitated art.

Come on, he urged. *Dinner is served.* And yet Korrigan was still just circling. Whatever it was, it was obviously smart enough to be wary of a second free lunch.

Finally, Korrigan stopped looking for the gift horse's mouth. It grasped the body by the wrists and dragged it back the way it had come from.

Charlie still didn't move a muscle. He didn't really relax until he saw Korrigan rip a jagged strip of skin from the dead boy's face and slurp it down like a torn lasagna noodle.

Korrigan didn't stop for another snack. It kept receding until it finally disappeared from the range of the night vision goggles.

Charlie stayed where he was even after the creature was long gone.

Charlie did not think of his killing side as a separate personality, but he did not consider it to be a part of himself either. It was more like a poison tide inside of him, a toxic blight that would rise in his brain and then recede, leaving only death in its wake.

This time, when the tide ran out, it left an idea on the lifeless shore of his mind.

- - -

"I'm telling you, something's changed," Waters said.

"You can't say something's changed when you can't prove there was something happening in the first place," one of the other cops said.

"Bullshit," Waters scowled. Waters, who was divorced, had no kids, supported the Cavaliers and the Browns, and insisted on miring himself in the darkest aspects of police work even in a community with so few dark aspects.

"You're changing the facts to match a perp that doesn't exist," Charlie said. "That's how cops drive themselves crazy." Except Charlie was smiling. And why shouldn't he? Charlie had no problems finding someone young and pretty to pass a Saturday night with; he rooted for the Yankees in baseball and the Heat in basketball; and, best of all, he'd found a corpse disposal site that was better than any quarry or landfill.

"In six months, we had seven dead bodies in a three county area. You think that's nothing?"

"I'm just saying I don't think it's one guy," Charlie said. He wasn't alone, none of the backcountry cops who got together to swap stories agreed with Waters serial killer theory.

"How many psychos you think we have out here?" Waters insisted stubbornly.

"I'm just saying, it's not even like the victims have anything in common," Charlie said.

"So he's a killer of opportunity," Waters said. "It's not the victims that matter to this psycho, he just likes killing."

"Waters, you can't just say that like it's fact," Charlie maintains. "You don't have any evidence."

"That's what scares me."

"What?"

"I don't think there's going to be any more evidence."

"That's convenient," one of the other cops chuckled. Or, at least, he tried to chuckle. Whether you believed him or not, there was something unsettling about Waters' conviction.

"I mean that in the last two months we haven't had any more murders, but we've had seven disappearances. We've got more missing people and less bodies. That tells me that whoever this guy is, and he *is* real, he's found someplace to hide his dirty work where no one else is ever going to find them. That means we're counting on a fifteen-man police force to get lucky enough to catch this guy in the act... otherwise he's never going to stop."

A hush fell over the table. Once again, Waters morbid frame of mind had derailed what was supposed to be a fun night of swapping ticket stories.

Charlie finished his drink and stood up. "Well, on that cheery note, I think I'm going to go." He toasted the table with his empty glass. "Cheers." He left some cash for his drinks and deliberately left a couple more dollars that he hoped would wind up going towards Waters' tab.

Seven. It was all Charlie could do not to stick his face in Waters' and laugh his head off. *Seven? Seven?! Try thirteen! I've killed thirteen people in less than two months and you're right, Waters. You will never, EVER find any of them. And guess what? Tonight it's going to be fourteen and you won't find that one either!*

– – –

Charlie pulled his truck over to the same spot he always did. He was whistling as he went around to the bed of the truck. He opened the truck gate and grabbed the body inside by the ankles. He grunted as he pulled it out. The corpse inside was heavier than his usual fare by a good hundred pounds but, after his conversation with Waters, he felt like Korrie deserved a treat.

He was starting to regret it now. Fuck, this guy was heavy. Charlie had to drag the bloated body out one grisly inch at a time. He gritted his teeth. Pulled. Gritted his teeth. Pulled. It was nearly there.

Nettled fur brushed against his bare calves. Charlie screamed and whirled around.

Korrigan was right there. *Right there behind him.* Charlie realized it must have come up while he'd been wrestling the body from the truck bed. So quiet that its claws could have been buried in his spinal cord before he even realized it was there.

Now it sat there quietly on its haunches in plain view of the road, looking as obedient as a inadvertently trained mountain lion.

Don't you be stupid enough to think for even a second that that's true. That fucking freak monster could still kill you any time it wanted. The only thing you know for sure is... you fed the animals. You did what your father told you not to do when you were a kid camping and what the Academy trained you to keep other people from doing. You don't feed the animals because they stop wanting to hunt on their own. Nobody turns down a free lunch and if any animal, be it a harmless raccoon or a 800-pound grizzly bear, knows where it can show up and fill up, no fuss no muss, then they just keep coming back. It probably recognizes the sound of your truck like you'd recognize a dinner bell.

A memory rose in Charlie's mind of a dog he'd had as a boy. His mother told Charlie not to feed her scraps but of course he would. For awhile the dog would wait patiently when she saw a morsel of meat in Charlie's hand, but if he waited too long it would jump up and put its front paws on his chest and-

Charlie hauled on the fat man's corpse, suddenly light as a feather, and dragged it off the truck gate.

The creature dove on the corpse the second it hit the dirt. It didn't drag the corpse back to its den. It sprang on it right there, ripped the dead body's belly open from hip to hip and dove fangs first into the steaming nest of intestines. Watching the creature feast made Charlie understand just how pitiful and amateurish the things he could do with a knife really were.

It also terrified him to the depths of his person. The core where he was not a murderer but a quaking creature of flesh that could tear far too easily.

Charlie stepped back towards the driver's seat. He didn't want to run but he was very much prepared to do so if Korrigan showed even the slightest sign of wanting seconds.

He didn't have to worry. It never looked up.

The creature was entirely focused on devouring the meal Charlie had brought for it. It didn't need to speak for Charlie to realize it would be eagerly anticipating the next one.

- - -

His neighbor Phil was setting up his lawn sprinkler when Charlie pulled into his driveway after work the next day. "Charlie!"

"Evening, Phil," he said without looking at him. Charlie was civil with Phil, but only because butchering his neighbor would land him on the suspect list by default.

"Going out tonight?" Phil often told Charlie that he himself had thought about applying to the force when he was a younger man.

Phil was hopelessly nearsighted, shorter than a girl scout, and his voice conveyed about as much authority as a librarian's. Regardless, whenever he saw Charlie he insisted on passing a few words as if they'd weathered a race riot together.

Charlie shook his head. "Staying in."

"Really? What's the matter? They finally took your credit card?" He laughed. "The way you've been partying you must be spending money like water."

Charlie shrugged. "Yeah, I felt like changing my routine a bit." He looked around the block. He saw buildings. Street lights. Paved roads. The refined civilization of it all was comforting. "Started to see too much of the same people."

Phil laughed. "I know what you mean. I used to go to this Italian place but-"

Charlie cut him off. "Sorry Phil, but I really want to head inside. Long day. I'll talk to you tomorrow."

Charlie walked into his house and shut the door. Locked it behind him. He turned on all of the lights. He made his dinner in the microwave. He turned on the TV and opened up a DVR folder that was 85% full of programs he'd missed while he was out making his own programs. He settled in with a plate full of food that was more chemical than natural, turned up the volume on the TV, and smiled.

- - -

Hours later, he was asleep in that same position. The sound of overturning trash cans woke him up. He sat up with a jerk. The greasy tray fell off his lap and spilled over the carpet. He listened carefully, trying to keep calm, trying to believe that the sound was just some residual effect from a nightmare.

He heard the rustle of tin against stone.

The lights were off in the kitchen. Charlie kept them that way as he crept into the room. It was stupid, he knew how well the thing saw in the dark, but it certainly couldn't hurt.

He approached the window from the corner, trying to remain as invisible as possible, and looked outside.

Korrigan had its back to him. For the first time, he saw its dirty gray pelt in the almost daylight of the outdoor light attached to his house. It was rooting through the dumpster. Occasionally, it would place something in its mouth but then spit it out just as quickly, uneaten. *Of course it did,* he thought. *It already knows what it likes. And-*

It gave no sign that it was aware of Charlie. And that made it all the more terrifying when it whipped its head out of the trash can and looked him square in the eye.

Charlie ducked down behind the counter. He held his breath and waited. Thirty seconds. Three minutes. Fifteen minutes.

After an hour, with his legs completely numb from crouching behind the counter and his entire body thrumming from the adrenaline pumping through his body with no place to go, he finally turned around. His knees stretched painfully as he rose into a crouch and crested his eyes past the rim of the counter.

Korrigan was right there. Clinging to the window frame. Looking right into his kitchen.

Looking right at him.

- - -

Phil's hands were sweaty as he walked up Charlie's driveway. He nervously tried to dry them on his pants but it didn't seem to do much good.

It was the "something" that did it. When Charlie called, his voice was trembling, like he was hiding some great excitement. Phil thought that maybe Charlie had finally picked up on one of the many veiled hints Phil had made about firing just one shot from the deputy's gun.

Or, maybe... but no, Phil refused to even hope. At least, his mind didn't. But the stirrings between his legs indicated that his body was hoping that Charlie had picked up on certain other veiled hints that he'd dropped.

Phil knocked on Charlie's door. He meant to knock twice but the door flew open before he could and hands grabbed for his collar and Charlie yanked him inside with desperate desire.

Oh my God, Phil thought. *It's really going to happen.*

And then the knife stabbed into his throat and Phil wasn't sure what was going on, even as his blood sprayed across the foyer in a geyser from one wall to the other.

- - -

Charlie withdrew the knife and stabbed Phil again, angling the blade to slide through his ribs and into his heart. More blood jetted out and spattered across his chest. Charlie ignored it. He grabbed Phil by the arms and dragged him across the ground floor, heedless of the massive trail of blood he was painting across the center of his house. His only thoughts were of his old dog and of his new one. Of hot paws pressing against his chest and an impatient mouth waiting to be fed.

He reached the sliding doors leading into the yard. He threw it open-

And two long, hairy arms reached into his house and dragged the corpse into the darkness of the backyard.

Charlie quickly flung the door shut again and locked it. But not so quick that he couldn't hear the sounds of the creature feasting from outside.

The locked door didn't seem like enough. Charlie staggered back without turning his eyes away from the glass doorway. He was so focused on the sliding door that he didn't even consider his footing until he'd already slipped in the blood slick.

There was no hope of regaining his balance. Both of his feet flew completely out from under him. His head struck the bloody tile with force that he couldn't possibly hope to prepare for and, even as his consciousness dimmed, he only had one hope. He hoped that he would not awaken to find parts of himself missing and the Tombely's Lake Monster crouched on his chest.

- - -

He did not wake until morning.

And when he did, all of his pieces were intact.

Despite what he'd thought before, he was not so grateful once he sat up and realized how much blood was splattered across the white interior of his house.

"Oh fuck," he said. "Fuck, fuck, fuck, SHIT!"

He changed his clothes and ran out into his backyard.

More blood there. The wood porch was soaked in it. He ran his hands through his hair, not realizing that the blood sticking to his palms would twist his hair into crazed spikes.

And then he noticed that the blood was not just spilled everywhere. It was arranged in a definite trail. Leading to the underside of his porch.

"Hello, Charlie."

Charlie turned slowly in the direction of the gate to his backyard. Waters was there. His hand was resting on his gun and, worst of all, he was smiling.

"Waters," Charlie said. He hadn't planned on it, but the greeting had sounded quite sincere. Someone listening to only the audio would not have suspected that Charlie was standing in the middle of an abattoir. "What're you doing here?"

Before Waters could answer, Charlie caught the curtains twitch in the house next door.

"Funny thing," Waters said. "We got a call from the neighbor this morning. Seems like someone painted your back porch red last night, Charlie." Incredibly, his grin only got wider. "Funny thing though. I stopped by your other neighbor's house to corroborate this, and nobody answered even though his car's still in the driveway."

Charlie's eyes went again to the hand Waters had on the butt of his gun. That simple posture told Charlie all he needed to know about what Waters was thinking.

Somehow, Charlie found the ability to laugh and make it believable. "Phil's on a business trip, Waters. I drove him to the airport myself."

"That so?" Waters asked. His tone said he wasn't believing it. His tone said he was thinking about his mystery killer who was so smart and seemed to know so much about forensic countermeasures.

"Waters," Charlie said. "I'm not your serial killer."

"Who said anything about a serial killer?" Waters asked mildly. His hand stayed where it was on the butt of his gun.

Charlie refused to take the bait. His easy smile stayed right where it was. "I think a wolverine got ahold of a woodchuck and dragged it under my porch last night, but that's just going off of the racket I heard at about three AM." He cocked an easy thumb at the neighboring house where the curtains had twitched. "I'm sure Mrs. Wagner would have heard it too if she wasn't-" he turned his thumb into a bottle neck and tipped it towards his mouth in a parody of drinking.

The pantomime was perfect, but Waters still wasn't buying it. Charlie tried to laugh to set him at ease. He also spread his hands wide so Waters could see he was unarmed.

"I was just going to look under the porch and see what was left. Would you rather do the honors?"

"Only if you don't mind taking a few big steps back, Charlie."

Hands out and palms up, Charlie willingly took several large steps.

Waters still wasn't convinced, Charlie could tell. It didn't matter, Charlie had presented himself as too reasonable. Too much like the man he'd shared a patrol car with half a dozen times. All Charlie could do now was... wait.

Without taking his eyes off Charlie, Waters crouched beside the black mouth leading under the porch. He looked into the gloom underneath the wooden boards and then quickly scoped out Charlie again.

He was exactly where Waters left him, hands up and eyes innocent.

Still wary of any attempt at a trick, Waters stuck his head and shoulders under the porch and groped for his flashlight.

And that's when the screaming started.

And the blood.

Waters braced his hands against the dirt and the rim of the porch and tried to push himself free.

Korrigan refused to let him go.

"CHARLIE! CHARLIE, HELP ME!"

Charlie dashed forward. He reached for Waters...

And yanked his gun from its holster.

He stuck the pistol under the edge of the porch and fired blindly into the darkness.

- - -

In the end, he didn't kill two birds with one stone.

He killed three birds with nine rounds. The final count was six for Korrigan and three for Waters. Phil was technically a free-be as whatever Korrigan hadn't eaten was found beneath the porch as well and his death was all laid at the feet of this "amazing discovery."

The investigators were sympathetic. Charlie had been taken by surprise and if he hadn't acted, Waters would have been killed anyway. The scientists were more inquisitive. They wanted to know exactly what Charlie had heard in the night and if he stored anything peculiar under his porch and if they could take soil samples for further study. Charlie was appropriately remorseful with the investigators and he was respectful of the scientists and their flagrant violations of his property in the name of this "fascinating find."

Why shouldn't he be? He had nothing left to hide anymore.

When it was clear that the scientists hoped to work into the night for any trace of the creature they could find, Charlie readily accepted their offer of a hotel for the night. It was really the least they could do.

- - -

That night, he felt the itch again. He tossed and turned beneath the crisp hotel sheets, unable to sleep until he scratched it.

He shouldn't do it.

It was stupid. More than that, it was absolutely fucking stupid.

He went out anyway.

- - -

It didn't seem so stupid after he caught the waitress getting off shift. Standing in a dark alley, her body on the ground and her severed head in his hand, it seemed like the perfect way to celebrate.

He had won. He'd eliminated not only the only man who suspected he existed but also the creature that struck more fear in him than the threat of a jail cell ever could.

He didn't even flinch when he heard somebody knock over a trashcan on the other end of the alley. Their silence said they were still in shock and Charlie planned to cut their guts out before they could get over that first bolt of surprise. He turned around.

Korrigan was crouched on top of the dumpster.

It can't be, he thought, even as Korrigan leapt silently off the dumpster and planted itself in the mouth of the alley. *I saw its body. I saw them carry it away with half its head gone.*

He saw a second creature, identical to the first, weave its way out from behind the dumpster.

And then a third.

And then he realized he'd been feeding more than one Korrigan.

The three creatures waited patiently in the gloom of the alley.

They're looking at the treat you're holding.

Numbly, he tossed the severed head at them and the three Korri-gans (Korrigi? Why was he even thinking of this?) fell to fighting over it. One of them eventually seized the morsel from its siblings and bit into it with a crunch but Charlie was already picking up the headless body and dragging it towards them.

The girl he'd killed was small. Five foot ten, one hundred and thirty pounds. Excuse me, Five foot seven and a hundred and twenty pounds without her head. Charlie could tell it wasn't going to be enough to feed three of them.

They would need more.

They would need so many more.

SEAN MCDONOUGH

Sean McDonough is the author of 5 novels, three published short stories, and one season of reality TV. He lives in New York with his wife and two daughters. Look for him on Instagram @houseoftheboogeyman and on Facebook at Sean McDonough- Horror Author. You can also look for him at your local horse racing track or horror convention.

ABOUT THE EDITOR / PUBLISHER

Dawn Shea is an author and half of the publishing team over at D&T Publishing. She lives with her family in Mississippi. Always an avid horror lover, she has moved forward with her dreams of writing and publishing those things she loves so much.

D&T Previously published material:
ABC's of Terror
After the Kool-Aid is Gone

Follow her author page on Amazon for all publications she is featured in.
Follow D&T Publishing at the following locations:
Website
Facebook: Page / Group
Or email us here: dandtpublishing20@gmail.com

Beverly Kills by Sean McDonough

Edited by Jamie LaChance

Cover by Don Noble

Formatting by J.Z. Foster

Beverly Kills

Made in the USA
Middletown, DE
13 May 2023

29958622R00146